T

May *G---*
real good!   *T West*
02/21/17

INDEPENDENCE
IN THE OZARKS

Truett "T-Beau" West

Contents

INDEPENDENCE IN THE OZARKS

We four men leaned forward and carefully let the weight of the neatly-constructed red oak casket slowly pull the leather wagon lines through our hands. Mr. Scroggins had lost a lot of weight there at the end, and his body didn't add much to the weight of the casket. When he drew his last breath, I lost the very best friend I had in this world.

Seven years earlier, when I was but a lad of twelve years, he rescued me from those who intended to make me a servant. I was prepared to fight, and even to kill if necessary, in order to keep my freedom and independence. He was eighty-eight years old then, and except for his intervention, almost anything might have happened. I was almighty glad when I heard his strong voice ring across the yard in front of the house. They had come to get me.

"That's a stupid move you are trying, Deputy! You are not going to sneak up on that boy, and when he shoots, he isn't likely to miss. He's been bringing home meat for the table for several years, and he doesn't waste valuable ammunition." I was watching the Deputy Sheriff, but I had my lever action rifle trained on Bing Hodges. And he wasn't liking it one little bit. I side-stepped to my left, away from the deputy, while keeping my eyes on Bing. Bing was the straw boss for

Mr. Robinson, who operated a tomato farm and several other businesses.

It was a beautiful fall day in the Missouri Ozarks in 1884 when they came, and I had been busy getting things ready for the winter, things I had learned from Ma and Pa before they died of typhoid fever the previous summer. Mrs. Robinson, and the prissy-talking government man with her, had tried to talk me into going with them. They told me that a boy my age couldn't live alone that way. I told them that it was what my pa told me to do, and that he knew me better than any of them.

Mr. Scroggins did not offer to move forward, and they all saw the rifle he held in his hands, both hands in position to swing the rifle and shoot. "Now explain to me, Deputy, why are you giving this lad a bad time?"

Mrs. Robinson started to speak, and he cut her off. "I asked the deputy. I assume he is acting in his official capacity, and I want an explanation. By what authority are you taking this action, Deputy?"

"Now, you don't have any call to interfere with my official duties, Scroggins, and I don't owe you any explanation!" the deputy protested.

"Seeing as how you would probably have a bullet through your gut now if I had not intervened, you would do well to explain this matter to me. This boy is under my care and any action where he is concerned must go through me." I was backing up a little now so that I could put the deputy more in front of me while continuing to watch Bing Hodges.

The deputy seemed flustered, and he looked to Mrs. Robinson. "I'll let Mrs. Robinson splain things to ya," he said.

"Then tell me Mrs. Robinson," Mr. Scroggins said. "What's this all about? I have been watching over this boy since the deaths of his parents, as they requested me to do, and everything has been going quite well. He just started this term of school, and the schoolmaster tells me Rick is one of his most promising students. What caper are you folks trying to pull?" Mr. Scroggins sounded like the St. Louis lawyer he had been before he retired to the beauty of the Ozarks.

Mrs. Robinson's facial features betrayed her anger and frustration. Making a special effort to control herself, she addressed Mr. Scroggins in a strained voice. "It isn't fitting Mr. Scroggins that this child should live out here in the woods alone. Mr. Robinson and I have discussed it, and we are willing to give him a suitable home. We can use a likely house boy. We will train him to work and to be a productive citizen instead of living out here in the woods like a wild varmint!" With the last few words, Mrs. Robinson seemed to regain her poise and confidence.

Mr. Scroggins spoke deliberately, each syllable rolling off his tongue in a clear and resonant tone. "That's a very nice surrey, Mrs. Robinson, and probably the best team of horses in this part of the country. You need to get them started back to town so that you can make it before nightfall. Tomorrow, you might check the public records, and you will find that I am this young man's guardian. His father and mother designated me when they decided to expose themselves to the typhoid fever in order to help others."

I was liking what I was hearing, and learning things I didn't know. I still kept my eyes on each one of them, especially Bing. I didn't trust them for even a moment. And neither did Mr. Scroggins, for he held his position. Pa had told me that he made arrangements to have Mr. Scroggins help me with any legal matters if both he and Ma died, but I didn't know that he was my guardian.

When the Wakefield family down the valley had all come down sick, Ma had felt duty-bound to help. I remember her and Pa talking long and low about it with serious looks on their faces. Before she went to help, she sent my two younger sisters, Betty Jean and Lou Evelyn, to her sister in Springfield. Then when Ma took sick, Pa had a long talk with me, telling me all kinds of things. He told me that I had to remember all of it, to run it through my mind over and over again.

I asked him to write it down for me, and he showed impatience with me, something he almost never did. "Listen closely and remember, Dedric!" he spat. When he used my proper name, I knew that I must, indeed, listen closely and remember everything.

"If I write it down, you will depend on reading it from the paper!" he said. "Anything can happen to the paper. You will need it in your head for instant recall." Then he went to see after Ma, and I never saw either of them after that.

Mrs. Robinson was the kind of woman who expected to have her way about things, and she expected to leave with a "likely house boy." Bing Hodges would deal with me if I caused her any problems, and if I read him right, he would enjoy every minute of it. Her face turned ugly.

"Scroggins!" she screamed, "Don't think that you have seen the end of this! You will pay for this interference." She stalked toward her surrey with her arms waving while using altogether unladylike language. Her actions spooked the horses, and they tore the limb loose to which they were tethered.

"Whoa! Whoa!" Scroggins called in a steady voice. Despite his eighty-eight years, he stepped quickly into the path ahead of them, and they stopped. A mixture of respect and fear flashed across Bing's face. He hated those horses because he had such a hard time controlling them.

And now at the ripe old age of ninety-five, Mr. Scroggins had gone to his reward. We slipped the wagon reins from beneath the casket, and I walked back to the residence with his two sons, three daughters and a group of grandchildren and great grandchildren. We would wait there until neighbors had covered the casket with the rocky soil. A considerable crowd of family, friends and neighbors had attended services at the little Free Will Baptist Church, and many of them followed the three miles to the gravesite.

At daybreak that morning, I and some eight or ten other men had taken turns opening the grave with shovels and picks. His body was placed alongside that of his wife, who had died four years earlier at the age of eighty-nine. Their chosen gravesite, located about 250 feet from their residence, overlooked a long and wide mountain valley. A double marker was in place, complete except for chiseling the date of his death.

Somehow, I felt even more alone in the world now than when Ma and Pa died. The things Pa gave me to remember, which included a lot of instructions for just surviving, had occupied my mind and my time then. Mr. Scroggins had taken me under his wing while, at the same time, requiring me to do for myself and make my own decisions. Shortly before his death, he told me that he might have been more involved in my decisions, except for Pa's request that he give me room to make a few mistakes.

I remember Pa looking me square in the eyes with as somber and serious an expression on his face as I have ever seen. "Rick," he said, "You are an Ozark Mountain boy. Ozark Mountain boys grow up fast. They stand on their own two feet, and they don't take water from anybody. They don't let anyone take their independence from them. If you begin to want too much in the way of worldly goods, you will compromise your independence in order to get them. Your freedom and independence are more important than any prestige you may gain from owning stuff. Do you understand? If you don't understand now, just keep on thinking about what I'm saying."

He went on to explain that if he didn't come back from caring for Ma, he believed I had what it took to make it on my own. He advised me to continue making the house my home and to do all the things to survive that I had already learned to do. He cautioned me against trusting friendly-acting people who talked a lot, especially if they wanted to do something for me. "You can make it without anyone's help so long as you stay well and healthy. Don't accept anybody's help. Don't let yourself become beholden to any man or woman," he instructed.

"Earn some money where you can," he said, "but don't spend any more than you must. The time will come when you will need it for something like a new wagon. Mules and horses sometimes die or get injured unexpectedly."

He paused for a few moments like he might be weighing what to tell me next. "It's better to earn money by producing and selling something than to help someone else produce and sell. You know how to trap and how to keep bees. You know how to make baskets, chairs and chair bottoms. Make sure you are paid a fair price for what you produce --- no more than that, just a fair price. Keep your eyes open for what people need and are willing to pay good money for."

Pa left walking. I thought he would ride Dan, our roan gelding, but he couldn't be sure that I would get the horse back if he died. I can still see him in my mind's eye as he went out of sight around the bend. I began to run through my mind all the things he had told me so I wouldn't forget even one thing.

"Stay in contact with Betty Jean and Lou Evelyn, and be sure that they don't want for anything. This is a good farm. Remember that they share equally with you." All his instructions kept ringing in my ears as if he was there in front of me telling me again, over and over. "Get all the schooling you can, but remember that your most important learning will come outside the schoolroom. Mr. Scroggins can teach you a lot, and he will do it gladly. Learn from him."

A grandchild walked into the house and announced, "The grave is filled and rounded up. It's ready for us to see it and put the flowers on it."

As the family gathered around the grave, I stood by myself, apart from the others, and looked across the valley. I felt very much alone. I knew that I had an abundance of friends, but I felt alone. Yet, being alone wasn't altogether bad. I needed my time with just the sounds of nature and my own thoughts and dreams. My dreams? What did I really want from the future?

Someone was standing behind me and to my right, but I did not turn. I waited for whoever it was to speak. The familiar feminine voice startled me a bit. "Are you feeling alone, Rick? I know Grampa has been a major part of your life." Her voice was soothing but vibrant. And she had read me like a book.

I turned to face Brenda Ann, a great-granddaughter. She visited her great grandfather frequently and had stayed with him during the last weeks of his life. She was only a year younger than I, ripe marrying age for young women. She and I enjoyed long conversations, and we each seemed to have a special feeling for the other. But I knew that it could never come to more than it was now.

To begin with, I had to think of Betty Jean and Lou Evelyn. In many ways they had suffered more than I had from being orphaned. The adjustment to city life in Springfield was tough on them for the first couple of years. Then, with the help of their older cousins, two teenage girls, they began to like the opportunities not available way out in the hills. Aunt Carrie had been good to them, especially to Lou Evelyn, the youngest, because she reminded her so much of Ma.

Betty Jean was seventeen and very serious about a beau who rubbed me the wrong way. I tried to allow for his being a city man, but he still seemed counterfeit and manipulative. It really worried me that she might actually marry this smooth-talking glad hander. I tried to set aside my prejudice against his soft hands and light muscles, but he didn't even know how to skin a coon or milk a cow.

Lou Evelyn, at sixteen, had more interest in the family farm and the beauty of the Ozarks. Insofar as I knew, she had shown no interest in boys, but I knew that they would be looking at her. She was a likely looking lass, tall and slender with big green eyes and light brown hair, but she didn't give her appearance the same attention that Betty Jean gave to hers. That might change in the next year or two.

11

I looked at Brenda Ann and our eyes held for long and satisfying moments. "Well, I have spent a lot more time alone than most folks," I said. "Somebody once told me that if you can't enjoy your own company, you shouldn't expect anyone else to like it?"

"I enjoy your company, Rick. I like it a lot." There it was, just plain and simple. That was Brenda Ann's way. Not to say that she was simple. Far from it. She just didn't care for drama and coy little games. A man would always know exactly where he stood with her, but I knew that man couldn't be me.

Her daddy was a Springfield business man. He moved there from St. Louis. Brenda Ann had attended the best schools, and she knew about high society. Not only did I not know about fancy gatherings, but I didn't care to know. I would make a poor escort to one of those high-brow shindigs.

Caught off balance, I could only mutter a word of thanks and "I enjoy your company too. I like it a lot." Then I wished I had not added that last part about liking her company a lot, even though it was true. The words just jumped out of my mouth unexpectedly. One of the things my Daddy told me repeatedly was, "When you start a thing Rick, finish it. If you can't finish it, don't start it." In fact, that was one of the last things he had said to me.

Now it looked like I was about to start something I couldn't finish. I just plainly was not in her class. A woman will get fascinated by something or someone different from what she is accustomed to. I don't count myself any kind of authority on women, but that much I had noticed. As much as I liked her, I couldn't see myself giving up my independence to jump through hoops in order to fit into the world that she knew. And that would surely follow if I let myself be drawn in by her charms.

Whew!!! I shouldn't have thought that thought. Charms? She had them, and they were real. There was nothing fake about her. I had to get away. Quick! She was looking at me like she expected me to say more.

I began to move past her. "Thank you, Brenda Ann. Thank you for caring. I better help Widow Phillips hitch up her mules." I felt really terrible about cutting her off that way, but I just couldn't afford to start something that I couldn't finish. She could plainly see that two other men were already handling that job for the widow.

My ride back home was a thoughtful one. The roan gelding Pa left me was getting old, and I always let him take it easy when we went places. The steep climbs taxed his strength, and a body didn't go anywhere in the Ozarks without climbing steep slopes. For the past two years I had worked with a foal I had gotten cheap because his mother had died from complications of delivery. I felt a kinship with him because he had been orphaned.

Spring was coming on strong, and it was a busy time of the year. Living in the Ozarks called for a wide variety of working talents and abilities. Better than most, I could hold my own among the men of the settlements. Pa had taught me well, and then necessity had prodded me pretty hard at times after Pa was gone. I had to learn to do things without depending on a helping hand, and I came to prefer it that way most of the time.

I loved to read, and in spite of all the work to be done, I found time to spend with books. Mr. Scroggins encouraged my reading habit by loaning books to me, some of which I had difficulty understanding at first. He helped me with the difficult sections, and they soon became much easier.

Mr. Scroggins stayed well informed on current events, and people throughout the community looked to him for leadership. I mentioned that fact to him once, and it prompted him to give me a short lecture on leadership. "Leadership is not a matter of finding a group of people and offering to lead them in whatever direction they feel inclined to go. It's a matter of standing for what is right and prudent when they want to do what is unwise and foolish. True leadership, rather than making you popular, will often make you feel very much alone."

One point that he made came to mind often. "You need to stay informed and current on what is happening throughout the nation and the world. What happens in China may affect you in the Ozarks, but you don't have to leave the Ozarks to offer leadership. Leadership in families and small communities is much more important than leadership on a national level. That's where the real difference is made. That's where a culture is shaped."

I thought of the several copies of the St. Louis Post-Dispatch in my saddlebags. Brenda Ann handed the newspapers to me after I mounted Dan for the trip home. She knew that Mr. Scroggins always passed them along to me. I didn't know how much Mr. Scroggins paid for his subscription to the paper, and I didn't know if I could afford it. But I had to find some way to stay abreast of current events.

From time to time I would dig out the old yellowed German magazines Pa had subscribed to. He taught me a bit of "low German," and the older I got, the more I wanted to learn more about my German heritage. His father, killed in the war fighting for the Union, came to this country from the low country of Germany, thus the "low German" language.

The challenges of those first two years of living alone permanently shaped me, although I had quite a lot of interaction with others at school and church. The neighbors who wanted to give me special help soon learned that I didn't want it. Like Pa had told me, I didn't want to ever be beholden to anyone. People soon learned that I could do for myself. By the time I turned fourteen, everything came pretty natural and easy, even the cooking. When we had eating meetings at the church I always got compliments on my cooking, but I paid more attention to how heartily the people ate it.

I did let myself get beholden to Mrs. Scroggins for teaching me to cook. I had always spent most of my time outdoors, and I knew how to fry fish beside the creek over an open fire. I could also roast a rabbit or squirrel over a fire on a spit. I knew nothing about baking and very little about cooking on the stovetop. Mrs. Scroggins respected my determination to do for myself, and she persuaded me that she was just concerned about my health --- that she wanted me to stay strong by eating healthy.

A passel of women in the area would have given an eye tooth for the stove. Most of them were still using cast iron pots in the fireplace. The store-bought cast iron stove, equipped with eyes and lifters, had been something special that Pa did for Ma on her birthday. She was as pleased as a mama hen who had just found some grain scattered for her and her brood. During those last two years of her life, she had cooked some really good-tasting food on her new stove.

Mrs. Scroggins' thinking about eating healthy must have been right because I grew to more than six feet tall, and I could lift as much as any man I ever worked with. I always held my own in wrestling matches, and when it came to really fighting, I got the best of several boys who were older and bigger. An Ozark Mountain boy has to stand up for himself now and again. There's always somebody around like Bing Hodges.

And speaking of Bing Hodges, my first run-in with a grown man was with him when I was fourteen years old. I almost never went into town, but I needed some ammunition for the guns Pa left me. When I came out of the store, he was waiting for me on the right side of Dan, the roan gelding. His face was flushed red, and I guessed that he had been drinking. He held a quirt in his right hand and his left hand rested on the butt of my lever-action rifle. A vicious smirk played on his red face. Knowing that I was facing up to trouble, I set my sack of goods on the plank floor of the porch and stepped down to the ground.

"You ain't so smart as you think you are," he gloated. "A body ought not leave his rifle on his horse when he's shoppin'. I don't like havin' a gun pointed at me, especially by a shirt-tail kid who's likely to pull the trigger, and I've been waitin' to teach you a good lesson."

15

The quirt jumped in his hand, and nobody would dispute that he was expert in its use. People felt sorry for the Robinson horses because he liked so well to use it on their rumps. I didn't shrink from it, but jumped forward to meet it. I had never felt so angry. If he had brooded over a "shirt-tail kid" holding a gun on him, I had also brooded over the cruelty I had seen in his face. He had really looked forward to having a twelve-year-old boy to kick around.

As the whip wrapped around my shoulders, I grabbed the plaited leather with both hands and jerked the quirt from his control. He bellowed his rage and began to pull my rifle from the saddle boot as Dan shied away from him. Skill with a whip was common among boys of the Ozarks. We used whips in contests to see who could snuff the fire from a candle without disturbing the candle, or to accomplish some other difficult feat.

Quickly I gripped the handle and flicked skin and blood from the back of his right hand. He flinched, but maintained his hold on the rifle. Dan reversed his movement away from Bing and swung his rump toward him. He reached forward and out with his right back foot, raking the bully away from him. Even so, Bing managed to get the rifle out of the sheath, but this time I curled the end of the whip around his wrists and jerked. The rifle fell to the ground under Dan, striking him in the flank on the way down.

At this point Bing made a serious misjudgment. He tried to get the rifle at the same time that Dan raked forward and to the side again with his right back hoof. The hoof hit him in the face, and the rock-scarred shoe cut a deep gash down his right jaw and across the chin. But give him credit; he was game. With blood streaming down his face, he jumped from the ground and rushed me.

I danced backward and to one side while drawing more blood from his face with the quirt. When he threw up his hands, the quirt drew blood from his hands. He seemed to become aware of the volume of blood flowing from his face, and he stopped to feel his face. At that point, two men caught him by his upper arms and began marching him toward the doctor's office.

Several people had seen the altercation from the beginning, and no one blamed me. The episode put Bing in such a bad light among the townspeople that the Robinsons fired him. I suspected that the prominent scar down the side of his face played a part in their decision. They were prideful people.

Bing left the area, and no one seemed to know where he had gone. Several men warned me to keep my eye out for him. He repeatedly told people that one day he would "get that smart-alecky kid."

I had the satisfaction of knowing that I had lived up to Pa's expectations. He knew that I loved the fields, streams and farm animals, and he refused to condemn me to the restrictions of city life. His confidence in me motivated me to do my very best. Anything less would have been an insult to his memory. I had won acceptance as a man among the men of the hills and hollers.

Even though I could not see a future with Brenda Ann, I pondered finding me a good woman and starting a family. I wanted to first make some progress financially. Mr. Scroggins had introduced me to more modern and efficient beekeeping than the traditional bee gums. He had three new-fangled hives that were much easier to care for.

The Dadant family over in Illinois produced supplies for a better kind of hive, and they published information that would help a beekeeper make the production of honey a serious business. Mr. Scroggins encouraged me to constantly increase the number of my bee colonies, and a goodly number of people had begun to look to me for honey. The Dadant style hives made it easier to produce considerably more honey. One of my prize possessions was the hand-cranked extractor that enabled me to spin honey out of the combs and return them to the hives for the bees to refill.

According to all I had read, Ozark country was above average honey-producing territory. I loved working with the bees, and I was the only one anywhere in that part of the country to acquire the yellow Italian bees. They were easier to handle, and they produced more honey than the dark German bees that were everywhere. I was looking to become a commercial beekeeper.

On my fifteenth birthday Mr. Scroggins gave me a book titled THE HIVE AND THE HONEY BEE, and I spent hours going through it, becoming more and more fascinated with these little insects. I also spent hours reading The Bible, and I made a connection between the two. The Bible is God's revelation of Himself, and He also revealed Himself through the organization and work of each bee colony. Even without The Bible, an elementary understanding of the functioning of a bee colony should persuade any willing mind of the presence of an intelligent and powerful Creator.

I could see a financial future in honey production, and it would keep me close to nature in the Ozark hills I loved. It would take much time to grow the business, adding just a few hives each year. No, I could not see a responsible way to take a wife in the near future unless I could grow the honey-producing business at a faster rate. I had to think of my sisters. I owed that to Ma and Pa. They had counted on me.

At the end of the war, Pa, age fifteen, had left a German settlement west of St. Louis. His widowed mother married a man who moved her into St. Louis. His father and older brother had been killed early in the war while fighting for The Union. His only other sibling, an older sister, had also married a man from St. Louis, and his mother looked forward to moving close to her. My grandmother and aunt exchanged letters and photographs with me and with my sisters from time to time, but I had not seen them since the death of my parents.

Pa had met Ma on a cattle ranch in Kansas. She and her sister, only a year older than she, had been orphaned by the

Jayhawkers during the war when they raided the small family ranch. They survived only because they were holding a small herd of the family cattle in a secluded spring-fed ravine to protect them and themselves from the marauders. They then became partners with friendly neighbors, and she met Pa when he rode by looking for work.

She fell in love with the rugged beauty of The Ozarks when she and Pa, newly married, traveled through them on their way to visit his mother and sister. After settling the family estate with his mother and sister, Pa made a deal for the farm on which we three children were born. He and Ma returned to Kansas just long enough to sell her interest in the ranch to her partners. Her sister, Carrie, sold also and followed them to The Ozarks.

Their mother was an Osage Indian, and their father was Scotch-Irish with curly red hair. Pa was a broad-shouldered blonde, blue-eyed German. Out of that gene pool, I inherited deep green, penetrating eyes that sometimes made people feel uncomfortable. My hair was coarse and dark, with strong glints of red, especially when the light struck it from certain angles. Having learned that my penetrating gaze often made people feel uncomfortable, I had developed the habit of look-ing at them just long enough to make a point or to receive information from them.

I unsaddled Dan and rubbed him down while the two-year old colt hung his head over the fence talking to me. He was hoping for some grain. I had cut back on his rations to force him to browse more in the pasture. He had grown into a moderately large bay with excellent conformation and a per-fect white diamond in the middle of his forehead. I consid-ered naming him "Diamond," but that just didn't seem to fit. The unfortunate mare who gave him birth was a top quality Quarter Horse, and his sire was a highly regarded Morgan. The combination made an ideal mountain mount.

I had spoiled him, and he could be quite demanding. I guess that could be expected from a bottle-fed foal. During his first several weeks with me, I slept in the barn with him in spite of some bitterly cold weather. Spirited and high-strung, he took up more of my time than I could rightfully spare during this busy season. I had to work him through his spookiness before he would be safe to ride around the countryside, and if I didn't give him sufficient attention now, he might never learn.

I gave him an ear of corn and walked to the house. From long habit, before I entered the house I paused beside a tree near the porch. It was a matter of caution, but I also liked to absorb all I could of the never-completely-silent outdoors. It fed something deep within me.

I saw a flicker of movement on the road. Someone was coming around the bend, a woman. I remained motionless where I stood, and listened more than I looked. It was a most strange thing for a woman to be coming alone at sundown. All my natural leeriness rose up within me. During my years alone, I had developed deep suspicions about anything outside the ordinary.

She suddenly stopped and looked back, and I could tell she was talking with someone. She worried a bit with her dress top and then continued coming toward me. She had half unbuttoned the bodice of her dress and pulled it open. I knew that in the gathering dusk, my profile merged with the tree trunk, and they would have difficulty seeing me if I remained still. Fortunately, my rifle was in my hand.

How many were they? Then I saw another, a man moving from one tree to another, and I recognized his peculiar manner of movement. Bing Hodges! He was closer. I needed a better position.

A stone cellar, built during the war-between-the-states, was about seventy feet away. It served as a potato house and root cellar, but it had been constructed in order to defend against outlaws during that lawless period during and after the war. The approaches to the barn and house offered a clear field of fire from that location. A well-concealed exit about twenty feet down the slope kept a defender from being pinned down.

A large cedar log with the front side flattened, was positioned so as to absorb any bullets coming into the cellar. It was pock-marked from battles fought years before.

I slowly lowered myself to the ground and bellied toward the cellar, pulling myself along with my elbows. A bad word directed toward the intruders tried to come out of my mouth. I was ruining my best shirt and pants. Inside the cellar I had a good supply of ammunition and Pa's old shotgun. These preparations didn't come from my own thinking; they were Pa's instructions.

When the woman, a likely looking full-bosomed woman in her early twenties, got within speaking distance, I asked her to tell me who she was and to state her business. She appeared surprised and frustrated. This wasn't going according to plan. She looked for me, and I gave her no help. Regaining her poise, her voice carried across the distance in clear seductive tones.

"You don't need to hide from me," she said. "I've had a bad accident, and I'm all bruised up. My dad has a broken leg. We need help."

"I might be inclined to believe you," I told her, "if you didn't have Bing Hodges sneaking around in the woods along with you."

"Who? What? I don't know anybody by that name. What name did you say?" I believed her. Bing was probably using another name, and "Bing Hodges" was probably not his real name either.

"And there is another man behind you. Tell everybody with you to step up beside you, and we can talk things over."

She was still looking for me, but Bing had located me. Fire jumped from a gun barrel, and a bullet hit the cedar log above me. He had opened the ball, so he might as well know I was armed. Levering my rifle quickly, I put a shot where the fire had flashed, and a shot on each side of it. A loud grunt followed the third shot.

The woman was running back down the road in the failing light, and if she had thought to distract me by baring her breasts, she was showing a lot more now. She held the tail of her dress around her waist, white legs flashing, as she ran at break-neck speed. But I was looking for anyone who might be thinking to take another shot at me.

My two dogs arrived at that time from one of their regular rounds in the creek bottom, and they flushed Bing from where he lay behind a tree. He fired a shot at them as he retreated, and I put one above his head. "You hurt one of those dogs, Bing, and I will chase you to the gates of hell!" I shouted. I called them to me and let him hop back down the hill, favoring his right leg.

I felt that I might be making a serious mistake, but even so, I couldn't bring myself to cut him down. His silhouette was plain enough in the shadows, but he left knowing that I had recognized him. He also knew that I had let him go, not that he would give that fact any kind of positive consideration. He would probably think it a sign of weakness. I would sleep outside tonight, but not at the root cellar. First, I would scout around a bit.

The dogs left to me by Ma and Pa were already old when Ma and Pa died, but one of them lived long enough to help me train "Rusty," a reddish tan Feist. Rusty now weighed a muscular twenty-five pounds, but he believed that he weighed one hundred and twenty-five pounds. Either that, or that size didn't matter. He didn't back up for any dog. Now five years old, he was two years old when Mr. Scroggins gave me a Catahoula Cur puppy from Louisiana.

A former client brought it to him as a gift. He graciously accepted the puppy, but after the client went back to Louisiana, he gave the brindle colored puppy to me. "You must spend time with this breed of dog, and handle him with a kind but firm hand," he told me. "I would love to keep the puppy, but I frankly don't know if I'm any longer equal to the challenge."

Now three years old, with a shiny blue eye and a patch of blue on his hind quarters, he weighed eighty lean pounds. Strong-willed, as Mr. Scroggins had warned me, he nevertheless submitted to Rusty's leadership. I worried that he might seriously injure Rusty because Rusty would have died before relinquishing his dominant status as the older dog. Perhaps "Cajun" sensed the tenacity of the Feist and chose not to push it to the limit. Who can really understand the canine brain?

Many people believe that because we know all kinds of things that dogs don't know, that dogs don't know anything that we don't know. I believe that attitude springs from either gross negligence or unmitigated arrogance. "Gross negligence" is a term I learned from Mr. Scroggins, but "unmitigated arrogance" came from my mother. I talk a little different from most of the people in the Ozarks --- not better, just different. Ma and Pa talked a little different, and then Mr. Scroggins talked like the St. Louis lawyer that he had been for many years. A lot of Mr. Scroggins had rubbed off on me. A whole lot.

Animals know all kinds of things we don't know. They know when the weather is going to change long before we do. Reading THE HIVE AND THE HONEY BEE was a real marvel. Those little insects have an organized society that should be the envy of every orderly mind. They communicate direction and distance to one another inside the hive while using the location of the sun as a point of reference. Who knows what dogs know where we don't even have a clue? I respect animals.

I sent Rusty and Cajun to check things out after I moved back to the tree in front of the log house. I was ready with my rifle to protect them if need be. If anyone was still lurking about, they would find the trespasser. At my direction, they did a complete circle about a hundred yards from the house

23

and found nothing. After they came back to me, Cajun whined as if trying to tell me something, and then bounded away. Did he intend that I follow him? He did not stop or look back and disappeared from sight near where they had come upon Bing Hodges.

Rusty did not follow, and we waited together for his return. He immediately came trotting back with a large rabbit hanging from his mouth. Supper! He put it down in front of Rusty, and they began to have a tug of war to tear the rabbit apart. I had seen them do this many times before. They cooperated to catch the rabbit, and then they shared him.

There are those who believe that dogs can't think, but anyone who has observed two dogs work together to catch a rabbit knows otherwise. Typically, the rabbit will run in a wide circle. One dog will stay loudly on the rabbit's trail while the other will cut across silently to meet the rabbit as it doubles back. I seldom fed Rusty and Cajun; they hunted for their food.

The Louisiana man had explained that Catahoula Curs often make excellent squirrel dogs, and Cajun had learned quickly from Rusty with little training from me. I loved to watch them work a tree from opposite sides so that the squirrel could not circle the tree in order to stay out of view. If the squirrel moved to another tree, one of them would see it. Squirrels constituted a regular part of my diet in the winter months, with Rusty and Cajun eating even more of them.

Even though we had enjoyed a spread of good food at the Scroggins residence, brought by people from throughout the community, I had little appetite at the time and ate little. Now I was feeling hungry. Without lighting a lamp, I felt around in the cupboard and found some cold leftovers. I put them in a cloth bag along with a skin full of water. Locating a ground sheet and an old wool army blanket, I carried everything to a spot up the hill that offered a good view while being difficult to see by any intruder.

The dogs joined me and appeared to settle down for the night, but I depended on them to remain alert to any sounds or smells. I also knew that they had much better night vision than any human being. I ate slowly and enjoyed my food. Then I arose and followed a dim path about a half mile over the ridge to the intersection of the residence road and the main road. Near the intersection, Cajun emitted a low growl while smelling about on the ground. Rusty busied himself examining a sizable area with his nose.

Not satisfied that they had left the area, but knowing I had accomplished all I could safely accomplish by starlight, I worked my way by a different route back to my ground sheet and blanket. I wished I knew how many of them there were. There were three for sure, counting the woman. Bing's leg wound would discourage them in the short haul, but it would make Bing more determined than ever to do me harm. Was his hatred of me the only reason for their presence, or was there another motive?

After a restless night on hard ground with no pillow, I was up with the first light of day. Rusty and Cajun had already left on one of their canine rounds. Dogs stay much more aware and in tune with their surroundings than do humans. Before folding and rolling my ground sheet and blanket, I stood beside a large red oak tree and listened while searching in every direction with my eyes. After slowly shifting my position several times in order to sort out all the details visible in every direction, I carefully worked my way around the house.

Then I walked to where Bing Hodges had taken a shot at me. I found blood on the leaves, and I found something else. He had dropped a nearly new Colt 45 pistol. That told me that Bing was sure to come back. A good pistol like that was not easy for even a dishonest man to come by. I wondered who he had stolen it from. I would send it to the sheriff by someone going that way.

"Lady," one of three Jersey milk cows, and her calf were talking with one another. They each wanted breakfast. My breakfast would wait until after their needs were fulfilled and I had a pail of fresh milk. The pasture had a good growth of new grass, and milk production increased a little every day. As I walked back to the house, a pail of milk in one hand and my rifle in the other, the dogs arrived with another rabbit. I would share the milk with them.

Most people in the Ozarks let their animals roam the countryside, and fences were constructed to keep them out of growing crops. My German father had been raised to a different way, and he insisted on keeping his livestock enclosed in fenced pastures. He made an exception for hogs. Hogs multiplied rapidly, and Pa marked the ears of those who belonged to us with a "bit" on the outside of the left ear and a "split" on the point of the right ear.

Male pigs had to be castrated, preferably within six weeks of farrowing. The angry sow had to be tied or penned before that operation could be performed. There are few animals more dangerous than an aroused sow defending her suckling pigs. Sometimes the fuss and squealing would attract a protective boar with flashing tusks, and he just might force his elimination at the barrel of a gun. There were plenty more to take his place.

Three milk cows were necessary in order to have a consistent supply of milk. They gave milk only after they calved, and then for only a few months. I had to manage to have their calving spaced throughout the year. The male calves offered up a supply of beef, but I usually sold them to families with more mouths to feed. I still loved fish, squirrel and rabbit, and I managed to trap a wild turkey from time to time.

I paused by my tree, as usual, to look about and listen. Suddenly both dogs left their rabbit and charged toward a little used bridle path north of the barn. Their barking changed in tone as they got closer to the object of their attention, and I surmised that someone was coming with whom they were familiar. Nevertheless, I remained alert and looked about in all directions. It was Peggy Frances Marlow with her younger brother, Bobby Jack. She was the oldest of the eight children

in the Marlow family, my next door neighbors just over a mile north.

When she got within speaking distance, she spoke in a strong and cheerful voice. "Now I know how independent you are Rick Weber, but I brought you something good to eat. It will go really good with that fresh milk!" When she got closer, she lifted a white cloth off a pretty three-layer cake with white frosting. She surely knew how to get my attention.

She didn't give me time to respond. "I fixed you a big one because Bobby Jack and I are going to help you eat it." She started toward the door, twelve-year old Bobby Jack close on her heels.

"I didn't want to come," Bobby Jack interjected, "but Ma made me. She said it warn't fittin' for Peggy Frances to come over here all by herself. I wanted to…" Peggy Frances cut him off.

"You hush, Bobby Jack!" she scolded. "You don't have to tell everything you know. You embarrass me."

I finally got the chance to say something. "Well, that looks mighty good, Peggy Frances. I haven't had the chance to cook breakfast yet," I told them. "Have y'all eaten?"

"Ma was fixin' breakfast when we left," Bobby Jack answered. "I wanted to stay and eat. Ma wanted Peggy Frances to wait until the middle of the morning, but she was afraid you would be gone off somewhere." She was looking embarrassed, but she was trying to smile.

"I have some leftover ham," I said. "Why don't we go inside to the table and eat that along with the cake and some warm milk?"

Bobby Jack pouted at Peggy Sue. "Hot biscuits and butter with sorghum syrup would be better. But I do like your cake."

I got to noticing Peggy Frances while we ate, not that I had not been knowing her most of my life. My route to school took me right by the Marlow house, and we had walked to and from school together during school terms. We had even ridden double on Dan when the weather was bad. But I had not noticed how she had grown into a really fine-looking woman from the top of her head to the bottom of her feet.

She was just two months younger than me, and most girls were hitched up and making a home at her age. A thought came to mind, and I asked her, "What's your Pa doing to-day?"

She seemed a bit surprised at my question, but she answered me straight enough. "He left yesterday for Springfield with Uncle Jess, and they'll be gone for at least seven days. They're thinking about buying a heavy wagon and startin' a freight line from here to Springfield."

That explained her presence here this morning. Her daddy wouldn't let her get close to any young men, and it had become a topic of conversation in the community. With seven younger siblings and another one coming every couple of years, it had become plain that her daddy wanted to keep her around to help care for them.

With her looks and pleasant personality, she would get plenty of attention from young men in the area if they could only get past Mr. Marlow. He was a big rough-talking man, but Peggy Frances was tender-hearted and kind like her mother. I didn't want to presume too much, and I didn't want to say anything to hurt Peggy Frances, but I could see this shaping up to another situation that I might not be able to finish.

When we finished our generous slices of cake, I turned to Bobby Jack. "There are two big rocks with bowl-shaped holes in them near the south end of the porch. How about taking the rest of this milk and divide it for the two dogs?"

He headed for the door with the milk, and I motioned for Peggy Frances to follow me to the door. We stood just outside

28

the door on the porch while Bobby Jack wandered down to the horse lot to look at the young stallion. I had not yet let him out to pasture. Peggy Frances looked at me knowingly.

"All the people at church and everywhere know that Pa won't let me get near a man, and I'm going to be in trouble when Pa gets back, because Bobby Jack can't keep a secret. I've always liked you, Rick, and I'm ready to have a home of my own. That's why I took a chance and came to see you. I didn't intend to just blurt it out like that, but I could tell that you knew. You were always knowing that way." She wasn't begging; she was just rolling it out.

"Peggy Frances, you have every right to be courted and to take your pick of the men who show an interest in you. You are a rarely appealing woman. Believe me. I know it's rough for you, but don't let your pa cheat you out of being able to look around and find the one you really want. I'm not ready to get hitched up. I've got to look out for my sisters first." She looked let down, but I saw something else come across her face.

She stood up a little straighter and took a deep breath. "Thank you, Rick," she said. "You always had a way of picking me up when I was down."

A thought was crossing my mind, and I didn't know how she would take it. After all, I was the one she had come to see. "In years gone by you and I have worked together pretty good on some things, Peggy Frances. Would you let me see if I can help you work past your pa? I have noticed that Toby Barrett likes you a lot. Maybe I could talk to him and arrange something." Her eyes lit up, and I knew I had hit pay dirt.

"No! Don't go over that fence, Bobby Jack!" I yelled. "He's not completely broke yet. He might hurt you."

He stepped back on the ground. "He's a pretty horse. I wish I could ride him."

"I have to work with him a lot more," I told him. "Maybe you can ride him some day. And maybe not. We will just have to see how he works out."

I turned my attention back to Peggy Frances. She was looking across the valley, but I could tell that she wasn't really looking at anything in particular. She was thinking. Turning again to me, she said, "You have always been a true friend to me, Rick. I came over here hoping that you would marry me, and I would have loved you and been loyal to you. But there has been something between Toby and me that I can't explain. And Pa is watching him like a hawk. I have been afraid to encourage him because Pa might hurt him."

I grinned at her. "And you weren't worried that he might hurt me?"

"No, not at all," she answered frankly. "Pa saw you stand up to Bing Hodges when you were only fourteen years old. And then he heard about you whipping that big bully that used to run with the Younger gang. He's almighty impressed by you."

"Well let me set your mind at ease, old schoolmate," I said teasingly but seriously. "Toby can stand his ground. I would as soon have him by my side in a tight spot as any man I know. I have wrestled with him friendly, and I have seen him whip a man who was bigger and supposedly tougher. You need not worry your pretty head about him."

I could tell that she liked to hear me say that about Toby. She was already thinking of him as her man and taking pride in him. And justifiably so. I didn't know how far she would have to ride to find another man who was his equal in character and physical abilities. I agreed with her to set up a meeting for her and Toby at my place.

She and Bobby Jack headed for home, and I realized that I had another threat to look out for. When Bobby Jack spilled the beans to his pa about the trip to my place --- and I, like Peggy Frances, felt sure he would --- I would probably get a visit from Mr. Marlow. I had never played matchmaker before, and I found it a bit exhilarating. I thought I knew where I could find Toby Barrett this afternoon without taking too much time from my work around the farm.

Toby learned blacksmithing from his dad, and he had become a topnotch wheelwright. A wheel on the Scroggins wagon that carried the body and casket to and from the church, had overheated just short of the Scroggins place on the return trip. The wagon had not been used in a long while, and no one had thought to grease the wheels. I suggested to the sons that they get Toby to look at all the wheels.

I had not worked with the colt for several days, and I decided to ride him to the Scroggins place. As I rode, I thought of Brenda Ann. I wondered if she would still be there. As much as I wanted to see her, it made me feel nervous and uncomfortable to think about it. I called the colt "Dutch" from the fact that his sire's owner was Dutch, and Dutch demanded my undivided attention. I didn't have time to daydream. In any event, I shouldn't be daydreaming about Brenda Ann.

By the time we completed the long steep climb to the Scroggins house, the colt had settled down and was acting like a genuine saddle horse. Brenda Ann was waiting for me on the porch. "So that is Dutch," she said. It was like her to remember his name, and I don't believe I had mentioned it more than once.

"I'm looking at one of the finest examples of prime horse flesh I have ever seen," she added. She stepped across the yard and through the front gate, and she walked around him as I tied the reins to the hitching post. I was not used to a woman showing that much interest in a horse, but Brenda Ann was full of little surprises. She stood in front of Dutch, not offering to touch him, and he bobbed his head at her as if he was as interested in her as she in him.

I heard some tapping with a light hammer at the barn behind the house. "Is Toby working on the wagon?" I asked. "I was hoping to catch him here. I need to talk to him."

"He has been here about an hour," she answered. I'm no hand at reading women's minds, but I thought I saw disappointment flit quickly across her face. It made me feel bad. I realized that it was very important to me that Brenda Ann not be disappointed. The realization jolted me. I found myself scrambling mentally. And emotionally too.

"Well, since you came to see him, I won't delay you." She headed back through the gate, her face turned away from me.

"That won't take long." I had to speak quickly, and it had to be right. "Will you be busy? I was thinking we might sit on the porch and talk a little while." What was I doing? What made me say that? Yeah, I had actually thought that, alright, but it was a brand new thought.

She stopped and then turned around slowly. A teasing expression lit up her well-defined face. She looked back at me and tossed her head to swing a lock of chinquapin-brown hair away from her brown eyes. "Well, I had planned to be busy, but maybe just for you I can change my plans." I knew I was acting plumb crazy, but when she looked at me that way and rolled those words off her tongue, I felt ten feet tall.

My mind was racing. I was trying to think clearly. I didn't know if I could talk, but my voice surprised me. It was strong and clear. "Good! I'll be right back!"

On the way to the barn, I talked to myself. "Dedric Weber, you've gone and done it. Started something you may not be able to finish. Sorry, Pa. I tried to do what you told me, but it was like I just couldn't help myself."

Toby looked up from his work, and a broad smile spread across his face. "Great to see you Rick! Did you come to spark Brenda Ann a bit?" His light-hearted chuckle helped me relax.

"Now that you mention it, that may be a good idea," I said. "But we both know she's out of my class."

"Now that I mention it?" he mocked. "Yeah, sure." He wagged his head and rolled his eyes. "Glad I could help you out," he said sarcastically.

"As to her being out of your class," he added seriously, "you need to develop some ambition. Some city gals take to Ozark country boys."

"Actually," I said just as seriously, "I rode over here to get you fixed up with the woman of your dreams." That grabbed his attention, but he looked at me the way a bridle-shy horse looks at a friendly-talking man with one hand behind his back.

I gave him a few moments to turn it over in his mind, and then I spoke just two words. "Peggy Frances."

He jerked like something had bitten him. And I'm thinking it did. The love-bug. "Out with it! Don't beat around the bush and don't play games! I would die for that woman, but I think she's still looking around." He waited expectantly.

"It's her Pa. She's afraid to encourage you."

I saw his jaw set, his fists clench, and I saw the anger in his eyes. I felt the need to calm him down. "In spite of everything, she loves her Pa," I said. "We need to keep things peaceable if we can. Come over to my place tomorrow, and we will talk over all the details."

"Peggy Frances won't be there," I added quickly. "We just need to calmly and thoughtfully put together a plan, and I told her I would work with the two of you. I know you have a ton of questions, but they will have to wait 'til tomorrow. I believe Brenda Ann is waiting for me."

As I started to walk away, I looked back over my shoulder without breaking stride. "Besides, you have work to do. You need to do it right, so you need to keep your mind on your work."

"A fine friend you are," he snorted. "You push me off a waterfall into a pool of swirling water, and you tell me to be calm while you go about your business."

"See you in the morning," I answered without looking back.

MORE PROBLEMS

I knew that I should have left in time to ride back before nightfall. Dutch was not ready for night riding in the Ozarks, or I didn't believe so at least. But who knows? They might have gotten me for sure in good light. There was no way to put the words of Brenda Ann out of my mind. Nor did I want to. Thinking of a woman when a man should have his mind on things immediately at hand can get him killed, and it almost got me.

When Brenda Ann invited me to supper with the statement that she would like for her daddy to get to know me better, I just couldn't refuse. Mr. Ashley guided the conversation in a way that enabled him to learn a lot about me without seeming to pry. He was clearly fascinated with the fact that I had made my way alone since I was twelve. At the end of our conversation, he said he understood why Mr. Scroggins had so much confidence in me.

I knew Brenda Ann's mother pretty well already, she being a favorite granddaughter. I left with the warm feeling that they both approved of my visit with their daughter. They invited me to visit them in Springfield, and although that invitation pleased me, it worried me. I would feel like a fish out of water.

About a quarter of a mile before I would have turned right onto my private road, the main road narrowed. To the left lay a steep precipice that leveled out a bit about seventy feet down. To the right, the mountainside was almost vertical. Broken clouds dimmed the starlight and made the shadows do strange things. That's where they ambushed me.

When the man-like shadow lurched into the road, Dutch reared backward and I thought he was going all the way. Desperately I managed to kick backwards and get my feet out of the stirrups, but I couldn't get them under me as I fell. I anticipated the rocky surface and rolled my head forward toward my chest in an effort to protect it. I did not anticipate the small boulder on which my right leg landed as I fell to my right. When my lower right leg made contact with the boulder, I heard the bone crack.

I also heard a hoarse scream that receded down the precipice on the left. At least I was conscious, but a sickening pain coursed through my right leg. I realized immediately that Dutch's front hooves had knocked the assailant over the cliff when he attempted to grab the bridle, a foolhardy thing to try. When I attempted to roll to my left, the pain seemed unbearable.

Were there others? As if in answer to my question, a dark form approached cautiously from the direction in which we had been headed. Dutch snorted, and in the dim light I could see the ears laying back on his head. The man came stealthily forward. He was carrying a long gun in a position ready to use. My rifle was in the saddle boot, and it might as well have been a hundred miles away at that moment. It was time to run a bluff.

"Take another step, and it will be your last!" In spite of my pain, I was able to make my voice steady and clear. He must figure that I was hurt, but he couldn't know if I had a gun. He stopped and began making careful steps backward.

There was a sapling within reach of my right hand, and it gave me an idea. Maybe I couldn't do it, but I had to try. As

36

intense as the pain was in my lower right leg, any movement made it much worse. I rolled slowly toward the small tree, and I almost passed out from the pain. The thought scared me. If I could remain conscious, I could at least throw a rock, and there were several of those within my grasp.

I pulled with both hands and worked my way up by painful inches until I was standing on my left leg and holding to the sapling. I spoke softly to Dutch, and with some coaxing I finally got him in position to reach my rifle. The feel of the rifle in my hands gave me a solid feeling of security in spite of my precarious situation. As if reading my mind, a shot barked a tree in front of me and threw shreds of bark on me.

Dutch flinched, but held steady. It made me feel really proud of him. He made a big target, and I knew the shot might have been intended for him. I didn't know how badly my leg was broken, and I didn't want to bring on an amputation. But that danger would become moot if I didn't make it out of this ambush. "Moot" was another word I had learned from Mr. Scroggins.

I leaned on Dutch, hoping he wouldn't move. I put the rifle back into the saddle boot. I could see nothing positive about staying where I was, and I had to trust Dutch to take me to safety. He, or they, might shoot me or Dutch on the way out, but I had to try. Thankful for increasing cloudiness that made it more difficult to see, I would not return fire. The flash from my rifle barrel would pinpoint my position.

"Steady, boy. Steady, boy," I said in a low tone. With all the strength I could muster, I used my one good leg and my arms to spring into the saddle. It required all my inner fortitude to keep from screaming to the top of my lungs. I am sure that the bushwhacker heard me moan, because another shot came my way. That shot missed by more than twenty feet, and that told me the shooter was firing at shadows. He couldn't see us.

Somehow, the weight of my foot with the boot eased the pain a bit. Regardless of the pain, I had to stay conscious and Dutch and I had to move out. Without my telling him or giving him any kind of signal, he began to move back toward the Scroggins residence. The sound of the metal shoes against the rocky surface of the roadway provided a target, and another shot whined by my ear, much too close for comfort.

Dutch struck a smooth running walk, a gait I didn't know he had. A mix of pride and gratitude welled up inside. As my foot moved to and fro with the movement of the horse, every movement brought throbs of pain. I used my left foot in the stirrup to steady me in the saddle, and I held to the saddle horn. Mt right knee pressed against the saddle skirt. We made a sharp turn to the left and put the mountain between us and the shooter. Even so, he tried one last shot.

Did he have a mount? Was there someone else who had been assigned to hold their mounts? Why did they attack me? Was my horse what they really wanted? Perhaps they were walking. Did they know who they were attacking, or did I just happen to be a target of opportunity? All those questions ran through my mind.

Mr. Ashley had warned me that outlaws were operating in the area, but that was nothing new. I had a measure of confidence that was largely unwarranted, because I had lived through such dangers since I was only twelve. With my mind on Brenda Ann, I just naturally pushed my usual sense of caution to the back of my mind. Knowing that she liked my company made me feel bigger and stronger than the biggest old boar bear to ever walk those mountains.

I realized that I was drenched in sweat. Fighting the pain took everything I could muster. I knew the leg, ankle and foot were swelling. I could tell that much. The boot would have to be cut away, but by cutting it on the seam, it could be repaired as good as ever.

Dutch, on his own, turned to the left, and I could make out enough of my surroundings to know that he had turned onto the road that led up the slope to the Scroggins house. In the poor light I would have missed it, but horses have good night vision plus a sense of distance and direction that lies well beyond the abilities of humans.

As much as I wanted to get quickly to the house that had meant so much to me over the past seven years, I brought Dutch to a halt. I told him that I wanted to listen a bit, and I really believe that horse understood. The sounds I heard were usual night sounds, and after a couple of minutes I urged Dutch up the slope.

There were no lights at the residence, but I knew they would have heard the horse. A gun barrel was surely trained on me, and my familiarity with the house told me where. I rode directly to that loophole. In spite of the darkness they would be able to see enough to know that there was a man in trouble. "Mr. Ashley," I said, "I've got a little problem. Been bushwhacked and have a broken leg. This is Rick."

The voice that answered was not that of Mr. Ashley. "Dad's a heavy sleeper, Rick, and I didn't disturb him. I will get him and we will be right out." Brenda Ann didn't act excited or upset, just intent on doing what needed to be done.

Then there was Mr. Ashley's voice. "No, I had not gone to sleep, Rick. Hang on." The front door opened quickly and both of them stepped out. Each held a shotgun, and they stepped in opposite directions as they came through the door. After first looking about, they met the horse as I rode it to the front gate. No effort was made to light a lantern, and I didn't expect it. Brenda Ann held the gate open, and Mr. Ashley directed me to the place where the porch had the greatest height.

Brenda Ann held the reins and Mr. Ashley steadied me as I dismounted. The pain made me break out in a new flush of sweat as I swung my right leg over Dutch's rump. I groaned and clenched my teeth. I hugged the nearby porch post as tightly as I could for a few moments until the pain subsided a bit. Brenda Ann tied the reins to the post and held the door open as her father helped me inside.

After getting me situated in the spare bedroom near the kitchen, Brenda Ann split my pants leg and cut the boot and sock from my foot. She grimaced, and I said, "Don't hold anything back. Tell me exactly what you see and what you think."

Mr. Ashley over-rode his daughter and made the explanation, which made me wonder if he was telling me everything. Then he explained that he had a little experience with that kind of injury during the war. "I'm telling you frankly that you may lose everything from about three or four inches below the knee. It's not the broken bone so much as the bruising."

He continued, "We will boil a piece of cloth and wrap it around your calf to stabilize the bone, but it will have to come off every day so we can watch the bruising and swelling. You are going to almost go crazy from having to lie perfectly still on your back with your leg elevated."

I remembered Pa telling me that I could make it alone so long as I could stay well. This was the first time in nearly seven years that I had been laid up for any reason. Pa was fiercely independent, and I felt obligated to live up to that standard. This was going to be a new experience for me, a challenge completely different from any I had ever faced before. In spite of the pain, all kinds of thoughts raced through my mind.

I thought of my livestock, the horses, mules and cattle. I thought of the young corn and the potatoes. I thought of the garden that was only partially planted. But the thing that weighed most heavily on my mind was my bee colonies, eighty-four mature hives and several starter colonies. This was the time of year when they required almost constant attention.

Willing neighbors would step forward, as I had often done for them during times of sickness and injury, but I knew of no one who had the skills to care for my bees.

I quit sweating and the moisture made me feel cold. Brenda Ann noticed my shivering, and she produced a wool blanket. "Mother has built a fire in the stove," she said. "We will have to boil and then dry a sheet." I was not so independent-minded that I didn't like her fussing over me. It was a completely new thought that carried with it a comforting feeling.

Mr. Ashley appeared again from rekindling the fire in the fireplace. "Rick, I'm going outside to ring the bell," he said. I didn't have to ask him about that. People who didn't have a bell would hang a plow share from the roof joist on the front porch and bang it with a light hammer or metal rod when they needed help from their neighbors. "We are going to send for the doctor. If we don't have someone at his office by daybreak, he may be gone."

I heard the bell ring three times and then pause. It was repeated twice more. When he came back, he offered me some whiskey for the pain. I politely declined. "I have never taken a swallow in my life, and I hope it doesn't get so bad that I have to do that." He looked at me thoughtfully.

I thought of Toby Barrett. Although he lived with his parents almost three miles away, I believed he would have heard the bell. I hoped that none of the people who responded would be waylaid as I was. I said a little silent prayer for them. In any event, Toby needed word that I would not be at my home tomorrow.

The pain had subsided a bit and I was actually feeling drowsy, when Mr. Ashley appeared with a large piece of a sheet. "We dried it over the stove, and it's still warm," he said. "It will probably feel hot on that bruised flesh, but the worst pain will come when I set the bone." He gave me a piece of folded leather to put between my teeth and a long roll of soft leather to grip with my hands.

"I saw a soldier hit a man on the head with a stick they had given him to grip. If you hit me with that roll of leather, it won't be so bad." He nodded to Brenda Ann and she gripped my leg with both hands at the knee, standing with her feet spaced apart for stability. The strength of her grip surprised me. He must have given her instructions out of my hearing.

When he raised my leg from the pillow, one hand under my calf and the other gripping my foot, I needed both pieces of leather and more; I closed my eyes and groaned. Ever since, I have been grateful for Mr. Ashley's knowledge and ability. I learned later that he had considerably more than a little experience with this kind of injury while in the war. The doctor couldn't have done better, and probably would not have done as well.

There was a surge of unbearable pain, and I heard Mr. Ashley as if he was far away, "Don't wiggle! Stay still!" Even though I didn't realize I was thrashing around, I tried to obey. The intensity of the pain had begun to ebb when he instructed Mrs. Ashley to wrap the sheet around my leg. Then came the burning. It felt as if Mrs. Ashley was wrapping hot metal around my calf. In spite of my best efforts, my shoulders came off the bed and I bleated like a bull yearling. I felt Brenda Ann's fingers digging into my flesh at the knee.

I was breathing hard, as if I had just sprinted up a steep slope, but the pain was receding to a barely tolerable level. Mr. Ashley had taken a dozen turns with a broad leather string around the sheet, and I began the long and very difficult job of simply lying still. Over the next several months, I would come to know Brenda Ann as I had never imagined her, and I would become as devoted to her as a man can be devoted to a woman. But right then, I had only the slightest idea as to the depths of her character.

She left my bedside and stayed gone long enough that I began to wonder about her absence. When she returned, she told me, "Dutch is in a stall with some water and a few oats in the trough. I rubbed him down good. He liked it."

There is no way I would have permitted her to remove his saddle, much less rub him down. It had already been in my mind to ask Toby to stable him, if he came. I was set to caution Toby to be very careful. That was one of the first of many lessons about Brenda Ann.

I looked at her with shocked eyes. "He didn't act up?" I asked lamely.

"Well, he seemed a little nervous at having a strange hand lead him to the barn, but I talked to him along the way, and he settled down quite nicely. He kept wanting to nuzzle me, and he liked it when I rubbed him above his nose. He's quite a horse." I whistled softly, and she looked at me with a puzzled expression.

I closed my eyes and concentrated on the throbbing pain. Seeing my clenched fists, Mr. Ashley again offered me some whiskey. "Not yet," I replied. "Maybe the pain will let up a little after a while." It seemed that the warm sheet had helped.

At intervals, seven men answered the bell. None of them had seen any strangers nor had any problems. Last of all Toby rode in. I already had some very definite plans for him, and he embraced them eagerly. His agreement gave me peace of mind, and I was able to actually go to sleep.

Truett "T-Beau" West

DRASTIC CHANGE IN CIRCUMSTANCES

Bobby Jack blurted out the news to him as he was unhitching the mules. Angrily, Marlow hooked the trace chains back and headed for the Weber place without even greeting his long-suffering wife. His rush to get there gave Toby Barrett ample notice because the bouncing wagon and the hoof-beats of the running mules could be heard almost from the time he left the Marlow barn.

"That's going to be your Pa," Toby stated calmly to his new bride. "The way he's going we may have another bedridden man to care for." True to his words, they heard the wagon crash and the excited mules continued up the hill. Both Toby and Peggy Frances began running to meet them. The mules were dragging what was left of the front axle and wheels, and upon seeing Toby and Peggy Frances, they began to slow.

While Toby tethered the sweat-drenched mules to a tree, Peggy Frances ran to her father. He lay on his right side, his right arm twisted in an unnatural position. "Pa!" she yelled. "Can you hear me?" Blood flowed from his thick-plastered black hair, and his eyes were crossed.

Peggy Frances put her hands on each cheek, and his eyes gradually came into focus after rolling around a bit. "What happened?" he asked calmly. "I feel sick. Help me."

"Help me get him up, Toby. I can't stand to see him like this."

"Not yet," Toby said. "Better not move him until we know just how much he is injured." He squeezed Mr. Marlow's ankle. "Can you feel this?"

"What do mean, 'Can I feel it?'" he bellowed. "Of course, I can feel it. Help me up."

"Just take it easy Mr. Marlow. It looks like you have a broken arm. We need to make sure nothing else is broken." After checking his ribs and making sure he could move both legs, they helped him to his feet. He complained again of feeling sick, and they had to steady him to keep him from falling.

His right arm hung limply, apparently broken above the elbow. "You have had a bad blow to your head, and you should not exert yourself right now. We are going to help you sit on this rock shelf until I can get my horse," Toby explained.

"I would about as soon accept help from the devil, himself, but it looks like I don't have much choice. If you hadn't stolen my daughter, I wouldn't be in this mess. This is your fault!" he accused.

"We will have plenty of time to argue about that later, Mr. Marlow," Toby responded in a steady voice. "I will go get my horse."

He saddled his gelding quickly and rode back. He could see that Mr. Marlow was talking harshly to Peggy Frances as soon as he could see them. When he reached them, Marlow sat sullenly, looking at his feet, his face set in a grimace against the pain he was feeling. Tears were running down the cheeks of Toby's new bride.

Toby dismounted and quickly placed his hands on Marlow's shoulders, gripping them firmly. "I want you to look me in the eye, Mr. Marlow, and listen to what I have to say." Marlow looked up angrily and started to say something, but Toby cut him off.

"Peggy Frances is my wife now. She had the right to marry me, and she did. You have no right to deny that to her. Now, listen closely and remember this. Don't you ever, not ever again, make her cry. Now I'm going to help you on my horse, and we will send for the doctor."

Peggy Frances had never heard Toby's voice so hard and flat, and she remembered Rick's words. "Toby can stand his ground. I would as soon have him by my side in a tight spot as any man I know."

She thought her father must have noticed that no-nonsense tone as well, for he made no response and meekly submitted to being helped into the saddle. She walked on the right side of the horse and held her father's right hand on the saddle horn to minimize the movement of his broken right arm.

Toby found a piece of newly tanned soft leather that was the right size to wrap around Marlow's upper arm. He tied it in place with leather string, and then put a sling about his neck to hold the forearm across his chest. Unwilling to leave Peggy Frances alone with her father, he sent her to carry the news to the Marlow residence. Her fourteen-year-old brother, Claude, would ride to town for the doctor. Before she left, he unharnessed the mules and released them in the lot.

The mules were hot and thirsty, and Toby moved them into an adjoining pen without water as soon as they had drunk a moderate amount. Fed by a strong spring, the water was cool and fresh. He did not want them to drink too much too quickly, although that was more of a problem with horses than with mules.

Toby remembered people saying that a person who had suffered a severe blow to the head should not be permitted to go to sleep, and he noticed that his difficult father-in-law was getting drowsy. He disliked the idea of making conversation with him, but he knew that he must. He began by filling him in on the details of Rick's injury, and from that subject, they began to talk of new outlaw activity in the area.

Toby was grateful for Marlow's interest in the outlaw activity because that was a subject upon which the two of them could readily agree. He seemed especially interested in Rick's encounter with bushwhackers and offered several suggestions as to their identities. When he got curious as to how he and Rick had reached an agreement for Toby and Peggy Frances to care for his farm while Rick recovered from his injury, Toby declined get into that discussion.

"You know, it would probably be better for Rick to explain that to you. I don't want to speak for him. I will say this: Being a good long-time friend of both Peggy Frances and me, he felt like we belonged together. He's more independent-minded than anyone I have ever known, but now he's going to be laid up through the busiest time of the year. He needs us." Marlow remained silent for a while, and he seemed thoughtful.

He looked more alert now, and Toby was not surprised when he said, "I don't feel sick anymore. Help me walk a few steps so that I can see if I get dizzy." After a couple of steps he said, "I need to sit back down. I'm feeling sick and dizzy again."

Toby kept a constant watch on him, fearing that he might fall out of the chair, even though it was a rocking chair with arms. A rider was coming from the opposite direction that Peggy Frances had gone. The private road to the Weber house made a partial circle, joining the public road at points southwest and northwest of the residence. This rider came from the southwest.

Toby's Winchester leaned against the wall by the open door, and Toby walked to the door while keeping one eye on Marlow. The horse had a distinctive hoof-beat full of energy, and Toby knew he would recognize it the next time he heard it. He was shocked and impressed to see Brenda Ann Ashley riding Rick's young stallion, and he was behaving like a seasoned saddle horse.

Turning to Marlow, Toby announced, "It's Brenda Ann Ashley. She's riding that young stallion of Rick's, and they look like they were made for one another." Marlow whistled and grunted in surprise.

She rode to the hitching rail and swung down quickly. She tied the reins to the rail and pushed Dutch's head away as he tried to nuzzle her. She took the time to stroke him above his nose. When she walked up the steps to the porch, he bobbed his head and pawed the ground with his right front hoof.

Brenda Ann examined Marlow's scalp beneath the blood-matted hair, and he seemed obviously pleased by the attention. She smiled at him teasingly. "A patch of that good-looking black hair is going to have to be cut close in order to take stitches and keep the wound clean. You have a nasty cut and a large bruised area. Don't try to cover it with a hat."

She reassured him, "The hair will grow back."

"Well, I am going to inspect a few hives," she announced, as she headed toward the door. "They are likely to be raising new queens so they can swarm. I will be looking to remove those queen cells so we can get some good honey production." A smooth steady stride carried her to a small building, and she came out with a smoker and veil.

"How about that?" Toby said to Marlow. "Rick told me that he knew of no one who knew how to work his bees. He uses new methods, and no one but he and Mr. Scroggins knew how it was done. Brenda Ann overheard him, and she declared that Scroggins had taught her as well, and that she loved working with bees."

Two horses were coming up the hill from the northwest. Toby recognized the steps of his gelding, and it turned out that Bobby Jack was tagging along on the other horse. He ran into the house and stopped short when he saw his pa's injured arm and the blood-caked hair. "Why did you get mad, Pa?" he asked very directly. "Peggy Frances is plenty old enough to get married." Embarrassment made Marlow's face turn turkey-snout red.

"Toby can fix the wagon. He's good at that." Then doubt began to etch his face. "I believe he can. It's tore up real bad."

Marlow and Bobby Jack shared a really tight father-son relationship, but it didn't keep Bobby Jack from seeing his daddy's shortcomings. In fact, he was probably the only person in the world who could point out Marlow's faults without incurring his wrath. And he never hesitated to tell him when he believed he was wrong.

Toby found Bobby Jack's statement and Marlow's reaction interesting. He decided that it might be well to leave Peggy Frances and Bobby Jack alone with their father for a little while. He had a feeling that Bobby Jack would bring his father around to a better attitude. "I think I will check on things at the barn," he said.

The sweat-drenched hair of the Marlow mules had mostly dried, and Toby gave each one a thorough currying. As he worked, he ran the events of the past several days through his mind. Rick startled him when he suggested forthrightly that he marry Peggy Frances, and that the two of them live in his home until they could build a place of their own. They could care for his stock, garden and corn patch. His oats were almost ready to harvest. Toby could find a couple of neighborhood boys to do that.

He had carried a torch for Peggy Frances for months, and when he learned that she felt the same about him, he acted quickly. Although still living with his parents, he had bought a small farm less than a mile east of the Weber farm. The old house located on it had rotted shingles, and it was no longer good for anything but firewood. The barn was still sound, although it needed some repair.

The fields and patches had grown up in bushes and briars, and long hours of labor would be required to put them back into production. The heirs, although raised on the farm, had moved to St. Louis upon reaching adulthood. Recognizing the rundown condition of the farm, they priced it to sell. Toby had his work cut out for him.

One of the first jobs would be that of hauling his blacksmithing tools to the Weber place for the summer. Earnings from that work would help him hire two or three young men to build a house. Most Ozark Mountain boys became pretty decent carpenters by the time they reached their fifteenth birthdays. He might need to find an older man to help him supervise them if he had a rush of blacksmith work.

As much as he hated to see his best friend bedridden, Rick's injury had opened doors for him. He said a prayer for Rick several times every day. People throughout the community were praying that his lower leg would not have to be amputated. Knowing how independent and active Rick had always been, he knew that lying still day and night while depending on others for his most basic needs would frustrate him to the point of sheer torment.

Rick hired a well-respected granny woman to sit with him and declined Mr. Ashley's offer to pay her. Ashley had returned to Springfield, but his wife remained with her daughter and a favorite female cousin at the Scroggins house. The family had plans to use it as a family vacation site in forthcoming years. They all shared the love for the rugged hills, fields and streams that had brought Mr. and Mrs. Scroggins to The Ozarks.

Upon completing the currying of the mules, Toby leaned against the lot fence and watched Brenda Ann, in her hat and bee veil, work the bee hives. He could see her as the perfect life partner for Rick, although he knew that Rick saw her as a city girl given to a completely different lifestyle. He had a strong feeling that this injury might turn out to be a real life-changing event for them. Brenda Ann, like Mr. and Mrs. Scroggins, just might love the Ozark way of life every bit as much as Rick.

He, himself, planned to maintain a good distance from the hives. He wanted no part of them. He watched Brenda Ann pry from the hives frames of comb covered with bees. After careful inspection, she returned each one very slowly to its place. From one of them she removed something that had the appearance of an oversized peanut. "That must be a queen cell," he surmised. She had mentioned that she would be removing queen cells to prevent swarming.

Toby had always had the impression that swarming was a good thing, but Brenda Ann explained that swarming greatly reduced honey production. Although it was true that a new bee colony could be started if the swarm was captured, both the new colony and the old one would produce little, if any, honey over and above what was required to sustain them through the winter months.

He noticed that she moved slowly and deliberately, and she used the smoker very little. Although he had no desire to have any dealings at all with the little stinging insects, he admired the patient and careful movements that enabled the success of those who did. He could see a similarity to black-smithing in that it called for just the right movement at the right time with the right touch.

Cajun and Rusty were running a rabbit in the creek bottom. Cajun's coarse bark was the only one he heard, but he knew Rusty was there. The way they worked together, Rusty was the one that cut across silently and actually caught the rabbit. Being smaller, he could maneuver more quickly when the rabbit tried to turn and dodge.

Cajun used his longer legs to push the rabbit hard, making him use all his speed and stamina to stay ahead. Given time and sufficient space, a rabbit would circle across its trail. A pursuing dog would have to spend time sorting it out when the scent suddenly went in three different directions.

Toby's natural interest in repairing wagons prompted him to go through the gate and head toward the house. He would let Peggy Frances know that he was going down the hill to inspect the wreck, but without letting Mr. Marlow or Bobby Jack know where he was going. The mules had settled down quite nicely. Already tired from a long trip, Marlow had whipped them into a frenzy and pushed them to the limit of their strength. The currying had helped to soothe them. They liked the attention.

A strong spring flowed from above the northeast corner of the residence, its location having apparently determined the location of the house. Years before, someone channeled its flow into one-half of a split hollow log that was mounted just outside the kitchen window. A baffle in the log produced a pool of cool water within easy reach of a human arm extended through the window with a gourd dipper in hand.

The water flowed to and through the lot, and a small pool had been constructed where it entered the lot. The mules had drunk their fill of cool clear water after he had finished currying them. Taking a gourd dipper hanging by a leather string from a stub of a tree limb near the baffle, Toby helped himself to several swallows of the cool water.

Seeing him through the window, Peggy Frances opened it. Speaking in low tones, he told her simply "I'm going to walk down the hill." She nodded.

As he walked around the corner of the front porch, the door burst open, and Bobby Jack asked, "Are you going to look at the wagon? Do you think you can fix it?"

Stifling a chuckle, Toby responded, "Want to come along?"

He answered by bounding off the porch without using the steps. The front axle assembly with one broken wheel, together with the attached wagon tongue, lay sprawled across the road. Bobby Jack surprised Toby with his strength as he lifted the end of the tongue. "We need to get this out of the road," he said. Toby was beginning to take a special liking to his young brother-in-law.

The two of them, with Bobby Jack struggling mightily, pulled the axle assembly from the road into the edge of a wooded area. Then they went to the broken and splintered remains of the rest of the wagon. They lay in the edge of the woods on

the outside of the sharp curve in which the accident happened.

Bobby Jack gave voice to what Toby had concluded earlier. "That low place in the curve followed by this hump made the wagon fly into the air, and it flew to the side into that Hickory tree. Pa was mad and he lost his head, something he always told me never to do. I didn't know he was going to get mad when I told him that you and Peggy Frances got married up."

Toby didn't know quite how to respond, so he said, "It's going to take a lot of fixing, but I can fix it. I just hope your Pa's arm heals okay."

They heard rustling of the leaves in the woods, and turned to see Rusty and Cajun. Cajun carried a large rabbit. "They caught it!" Bobby Jack said excitedly. "They ran a wide circle, and I thought it had gotten away from them."

"Cajun is a different kind of dog," he added. "I want some puppies from him. Our bulldog puppy will be old enough to breed in September, and puppies from them will make some real good dogs. There are some unmarked wild hogs on the other side of the county, and I want to catch some of them. We eat a lot of sausage, pork chops and bacon."

As they two walked back up the hill to the house, they heard a horse coming from the direction of the Marlow residence. "That sounds like Lucy, our mare," Bobby Jack said. "Claude rode her to fetch the doctor. He must have found him."

Soon the fourteen-year-old Claude appeared around the curve, holding the copper colored mare to a steady trot. Claude, a tall and slender youth, loved to ride, and he rode very well. As he started up the steeper slope, he slowed the horse to a walk, and Toby took mental note of the fact. One could size up a man's character by how much consideration he showed for his horse.

"The doctor is on his way," he announced. "I spotted his surrey at the Wiggins house. He had just finished setting a broken arm there. This seems to be the day for broken arms."

Back at the house Marlow seemed embarrassed by his predicament. He actually apologized to Claude for injuring himself and tearing up the wagon. "This is going to put an extra load on you," he told him, "until this arm heals."

Bobby Jack spoke up quickly. "Me and Claude have been handling things pretty good while you were gone. We can handle it."

Brenda Ann stepped inside long enough to say goodbye. She had finished her inspection of the hives. "I removed twenty-three queen cells," she said. "There would have been swarms everywhere in a short time. It will take another day or two to work through all of them."

"Will you show me how to work bees?" Bobby Jack asked. "Pa don't like them, and he don't want to spend money for honey when we have syrup. I like honey."

"Rick has another veil out there," she responded. "Maybe you can help me tomorrow. Do you swell badly when you get stung? It happens. I was stung twice today."

"You were stung only twice?" Mr. Marlow exclaimed. "They would sting me a dozen times before I even opened the hive." Toby could see his face set against the pain he was suffering, but he wanted to participate in what was going on around him. Maybe there was some hope for a decent family relationship with him after all.

As Dutch's distinctive hoof-beats faded into the distance, Marlow expressed his dismay. "Unbelievable," he said. "She comes riding in on a half-broke stallion likes there's nothing to it at all. And then she goes into all those hives like those stinging devils are good friends of hers. And of all things, she's a city gal." He wagged his head from side to side.

Toby and Bobby Jack walked out to meet the doctor when

they heard his mule and surrey. The biggest mule Toby had ever seen pulled his one-horse rig. Someone had mentioned that he came out of a Belgian mare in Iowa. "How do they grow a mule that big?" Bobby Jack asked. His curiosity never rested.

The doctor stressed to Marlow that he should not use the arm at all until it had fully healed. "You have bone splinters," he said. "Hopefully, they will reattach to the bone if you give them adequate opportunity. If you start using the arm too soon, even for small stuff, they will be left floating and will always bother you. Now, let me work on that hard head of yours."

When he finished sewing the lacerated scalp, he instructed, "You need to stay here tonight, and then walk home tomorrow, slowly and easily. Any kind of ride will jostle your arm, and you don't want that."

PRAYING FOR PATIENCE

My love of reading helped me pass the long hours of lying on my back. That and Brenda Ann. If a man had to recover from a messed-up leg, he couldn't ask for a better situation. I sort of wished that Brenda Ann would spend more time in the house because I loved to hear her steps. There was much to be done outside, and she took it upon herself to do it. I came to realize that even the large Scroggins house was too small for her. She loved the outdoors.

She especially loved to spend time with Dutch, and she would bring him to the open window so that I could talk to him. He seemed to understand my condition. The first three weeks were the toughest. The leg swelled terribly and ached constantly. People all around the countryside were praying that I wouldn't lose my lower leg. It looked as if gangrene was ready to set in.

In the fourth week it began to feel better, and for the first time the doctor sounded encouraging. He checked on me every two or three days, and I was wondering how big a hole he and Granny Stratton were to put in my savings. Not that I begrudged even one dime, because they earned it, especially Granny.

One of the problems of feeling better was impatience. I wanted to be up and about. Brenda Ann kept going through the Scroggins collection of books and finding some I really liked. I especially liked books of history, books that recounted the struggles of those who came before us. I gained a greater understanding of what caused the war-between-the-states and the role that Missouri had played in it.

I knew that the county in which we lived had suffered from bushwhackers, but I didn't know how badly the counties farther south had suffered, especially Howell County that lay against the border with Arkansas. The lawlessness that continued after the war helped produce a vigilante group called "The Baldknobbers" in three southern Missouri counties. Their rise was accompanied by further strife and bloodshed.

Mr. Scroggins had collected many books about the frontier from the earliest days of the colonies to the present. Those books may have saved me from going mad. The frontier had been a major part of United States history, and it was now virtually gone. The frontier had greatly influenced the culture for the better, and I wondered what kind of people our nation would become without the frontier influence. Men and women of the frontier learned to value independence and self-sufficiency.

The St. Louis Dispatch kept me abreast of current events on a state and national level, but I realized that what happens within families and communities is of much greater importance. Few of us have the opportunity to make any significant difference on a state or national level, but the cumulative effect of attitudes and actions of individual persons all across the land provide the culture in which we live.

I read about President Ben Harrison and his support for high tariffs. It was said that the high tariffs protected the farmers as well as the manufacturers, but I found it difficult to understand how the tariffs did more for the farmers than make prices higher on the things we had to buy. I did like most of what I read about The Sherman Antitrust Act, but The Ozarks were so isolated and self-sufficient that these economic measures affected us but little.

All information pointed toward President Harrison being a sincere practicing Christian, and that fact gave me a good measure of confidence in his policies. I had learned to put confidence in people who held The Bible in high regard, although I knew that many misused The Bible to promote selfish ends. Nevertheless, I believed in my own ability to make plans for the future based on what information I could secure. In the final essence, it is God who directs His children's steps.

Pa and Ma knew that I did not like to stay inside, even to the extent that I would stir about in near-freezing rainy weather. There was a peace about that kind of weather. Their recognition of that characteristic in me, led them to provide a life for me away from the confines of city life. Confinement to a bed for endless hours was bearable only because I knew it wouldn't last. I prayed for patience to make it through the enforced idleness.

After I got through the constant pain, Toby brought Rusty and Cajun to see me. He explained that they seemed to be depressed by my absence, especially after they smelled the pants that had been cut off me. "They need to know that you are still alive, even if you are not well," he said.

When they got to the house and Brenda Ann greeted them, I could hear their whines of gladness upon seeing her. But when she tried to get them to come inside the house, they refused. They were outside dogs, and they wanted all the room of the outdoors. I had never even thought of bringing them inside, even when they were puppies. In bitterly cold weather they slept under the house near the base of the fireplace.

When I realized that they were not going to respond to the urgings of Toby and Brenda Ann, I called their names and whistled for them. They bounded through the house and into my bed. Brenda Ann ran quickly to keep them from bumping my bad leg. "Sit! Sit! Quiet!" I told them. They obeyed momentarily, but then began to twist and turn again. It did me a lot of good down deep inside to see how glad they were to see me.

"No, I'm not dead," I told them. "Not yet, anyway."

Toby told me later that they both perked up a lot after they saw me. After that, on their own, they came to see me for a few minutes every day. I didn't let them get in the nice Scroggins bed again. They would sit on the floor and look at me for several minutes, wagging their tails as I talked to them. They would soon get restless and begin to pace the floor. I would tell them then to go home, and they would quickly make their way out of the house.

The month of June was wetter than usual, and I told Brenda Ann not to hurry about harvesting the honey until we could be sure that it had fully cured. We needed a couple of weeks of hot weather and low humidity. By the time we took off the supers filled with honey, I was able to help a little. I sat in a chair and spun the honey out of the combs, after first helping to uncap them with a hot knife.

But first of all, I had to make it from the Scroggins residence to my own. The doctor sternly admonished me not to put any weight on my injured leg. He told me that it would be a very gradual process of beginning with a very small amount of weight and increasing it bit by bit. To do otherwise would produce a crooked leg, and perhaps a new break. A neighbor loaned me a pair of strong and well-used crutches, and as I used them, I realized how much strength I had lost while lying completely still.

Brenda Ann brought my old gelding back with her on one of her trips to check the hives. Dan seemed as happy as Rusty and Cajun had been to see me. The next morning I felt like a small boy going for his first horseback ride. Again, when I tried to get into the saddle I was reminded of my weakness. With all my strength, I gripped the front and back of the saddle and thrust upward with my good left leg. My first effort failed.

"Got to get more of my arms into it," I told Brenda Ann. She was holding the reins for me. "I hope the cinch strap is tight enough to keep the saddle from turning."

The saddle horn gouged me as I swung my bad right leg over Dan's back. "Don't put your weight on that right stirrup," Brenda Ann reminded. "It's so natural to do that. It will be hard not to." Dan stood patiently, waiting for directions from me.

Brenda Ann had attached the saddle boot to the saddle. She handed my Winchester to me, and then I noticed that she had a saddle boot and rifle on Dutch. "I haven't trained Dutch to stand pat when a rifle is fired from his back," I told her. "You can't afford to take that chance. No telling what he would do."

She grinned at me, but I could tell that there was something serious behind the grin. "I've been riding with a rifle every time I went to your place since the first couple of times. I saw suspicious movement in the woods near the creek. Dutch will stand. And he wasn't hard to train."

"Well don't just sit there with your mouth open," she scolded. "I'm a woman, but not a helpless one."

"I'm trying to keep from falling out of this saddle," I answered. "First, you ride a half-broke stallion like it might be just a simple thing. And now you tell me you trained him to stand when you fire a gun from his back. Woman you do beat all! I may just have to marry you!"

And then I did almost fall out of the saddle. Somehow, being around Brenda Ann made me say things I had never intended to say. Words would just jump out of my mouth. It made me think of how my mother often paraphrased lessons from the scriptures. One of the many things she often said was, "Out of the abundance of the heart the mouth speaks."

I saw a twinkle in her eye. "You can ask me, but you can't marry me unless I agree. Don't take anything for granted."

Then she abruptly changed the subject.

Her face serious, she warned me of possible danger ahead. "I have seen suspicious activity along the creek since then, and yesterday there were three of them. I'm pretty sure they don't know that I saw them. They think I'm just a happy-go-lucky mountain maiden singing as she rides. I'm glad you are with me today."

She put my crutches across the saddle, and I tied them to the saddle horn. I pulled my rifle from the boot and checked it carefully. She mounted Dutch and did the same. I led out, holding Dan to a walk as I held the crutches steady with my right hand. The exhilaration of being back in the saddle had been dampened by the warning Brenda Ann had given. If I let something happen to Brenda Ann… I couldn't stand the thought.

I saw them before she did. She was probably looking toward the creek where she had seen them earlier. But they had moved to the other side of the road; at least two of them had. A third one moved quickly between two trees, and again, I recognized the peculiar gait of Bing Hodges, or

whatever his name was. I pulled Dan to a halt and turned to Brenda Ann as she came alongside.

Had I not glimpsed their sneaky movements as they got in place close to the road, I would not be able to see them now. They had each held a rifle and they were now hidden behind large trees. There was no doubt about it. It was an ambush, bushwhackers at work.

We were not yet within good rifle range. "I saw three, two on the upper side of the road," I told her. "Bing Hodges is on the lower side." I made it a point not to show any signs of alarm or to make any motion in their direction. Instead, I pointed upward toward the top of a nearby tree on our left and asked her to look at it.

"This will give us a chance to get our rifles out of the boots without their knowing that we are aware of them. But keep cutting your eyes all around," I said. I had a plan to go around them.

A fleeting thought entered my mind, but it was quickly dismissed. Should we, for Brenda Ann's safety, turn back? In the long term that would only increase the danger to her. They had gotten a good look at her all-woman appearance, and they would not now be easily discouraged.

Brigands such as Bing Hodges know they are not real men, and that awareness of their lack of manhood must eat at them. Although they can be viciously aggressive, they are cowards. They look for dishonesty and cowardice in others because it makes them feel better about themselves. If we had retreated, they would have gained deep satisfaction from that fact, and that would have encouraged them to come after us sooner or later.

"There's a trail down by the creek, and a bluff that will shield us until we get around them." I pretended to aim my rifle at the tree and then hurried Dan down the slope toward the creek as if I was pursuing some animal. Brenda Ann followed. I gripped my rifle and crutches with the saddle horn, and took care that the crutches didn't catch on a tree or bush.

We had bypassed them when suddenly around a curve of the bluff there was their camp, including nine horses in a makeshift corral. They were on property belonging to Mr. Nunn, and I knew that there was no way he would have consented for them to be there. As I leaned to untie the rope that held the crude gate, Brenda Ann was there on her feet. "I will get it," she said, and she made quick work of it.

As she opened the gate I rode toward the other side of the pen to urge the horses out. There was movement across the pen to my left. It was the busty petite woman who I had last seen running wildly with her dress tail around her waist. She had a rifle leveled at Brenda Ann and appeared to be taking careful aim.

It had never crossed my mind that I would ever fire a gun at a woman, but she had her gun aimed at Brenda Ann. Almost without my willing it, my rifle jumped in my hands. Her rifle fell to the ground as she screamed and clutched her right shoulder. The horses bolted through the narrow gate and Brenda Ann sprang to Dutch's back. We were off and running.

At that point the road alongside the creek was wide and open, a fact for which I was very thankful. It would have been most difficult to hold the crutches and go through bushes and limbs. When we got beyond rifle range, I slowed Dan to a walk. We had to turn up a steep slope, and he was already winded from the short run. His good days were behind him.

Nine horses would usually mean seven to nine people, but we had accounted for only four. A fifth horse would be a spare or a pack horse, but nine? A gang of seven to nine people could be real trouble. Upon getting the news Toby would get a few neighbors together, and they would do whatever was necessary to send the outlaws on their way. Just now they would be busy trying to round up their horses, and they would not likely get all back. That would put me higher on their list to take revenge.

It bothered me that I had pulled the trigger on a woman, and I hoped she would recover from the wound. Given a split second to make a choice, I had to remove the threat to Brenda Ann. Maybe it was my imagination, but in the fleeting look that I had, it seemed that her face was contorted and blazing with hate. Now how could that be?

When we rode into my yard, Toby came from behind the barn with his rifle in his hand. "Do y'all know anything about that shot?" he asked. "We have had some strange things going on around here." He was looking carefully in all directions.

"Cajun and Rusty ran someone away from the horse lot about four o'clock this morning." He added. "He has a hole in the seat of his britches now and a sore butt. Cajun took a bite out of his back side." He pointed to a piece of dirty blood-stained cloth hanging on a nail on the front porch.

One of your mules had a rope halter on his head and a sack of your corn tied to his back. I was able to find enough sign to know that there were at least two of them. They came in on foot, so I'm guessing they are camped fairly close by. I don't believe you have a neighbor who would try to pull a stunt like that.

Brenda Ann had dropped Dutch's reins to the ground as she dismounted, and I noticed he stood perfectly still. What she had done with that young stallion was almost beyond belief. She moved quickly to help me with my crutches, and Toby stepped forward to help me dismount.

When I got my crutches in place under my arms, I suddenly realized that my lower right leg was hurting, a deep throbbing ache. I must have put weight on it while my attention was on other things. I didn't mention it, and I just hoped nothing had happened to delay the healing process.

"Let's put our heads together and decide how to deal with this," I said. "We have some things to tell you. And we need to keep a sharp lookout in the meanwhile. Where are Cajun and Rusty? They can help us maintain a lookout."

"And Dutch," added Brenda Ann. "He doesn't seem to miss anything. We need to keep our eyes on him." Toby and I both raised our eyebrows. Now that was something neither of us had thought about.

My awkwardness and weakness in working my way up the front steps with my crutches, embarrassed and frustrated me. The time in bed had taken a lot out of me. Peggy Frances held the rocking chair steady while I maneuvered to take a seat in it. I couldn't help but notice that her face showed a peace and satisfaction I had never seen before. It made me feel good about the part I had played in getting her and Toby together.

"How is your Pa's arm?" I asked her.

"The swelling is almost gone, and the doctor says he thinks it's going to be just fine," she answered. "You may see him in a few minutes. He comes over almost every day about this time. He has decided that he's right proud of his son-in-law. Brags about him to all the neighbors."

"Yeah, I heard that," I responded. "It worries me a bit. Toby may get the big head. He may decide he is something special," I joked.

"Dedric Weber, if you start putting down my man, you may get another bad leg. You had better watch your mouth."

It was hard to tell if she was just bantering or if she was completely serious.

I put both hands in the air. "I give up," I said. "I learned years ago not to tangle with you. If you say he hung the moon, then he hung the moon."

"Look at Dutch!" Brenda Ann interrupted. His head was turned toward the direction from which we had come and his ears were cocked in that direction. Then his right ear, the one opposite the sound he apparently heard, began to rotate to help him catch any other sounds. Brenda Ann quickly walked to him and slipped her rifle from the saddle boot.

Holding the rifle parade style on her right shoulder, with her left hand she led Dutch to the opposite side of the house. That would put him out of the line of any fire from the direction to which he had alerted us. Toby did the same with Dan after he first retrieved my rifle for me.

Peggy Frances handed my crutches to me. "Better come inside," she said. "You're an inviting target here on the porch, and you can't move around well enough to stay outside."

"She's right, Rick," Brenda Ann added. "I'm going to the back of the house and watch for anyone approaching over the ridge." Toby headed toward the barn.

On my crutches I swung to the south window in the main

bedroom. It had been Pa's and Ma's bedroom, and now it belonged to the newlyweds. I could never bring myself to sleep there because it had belonged to Ma and Pa. It had the largest window in the house. A horse carrying double came barely into view and stopped.

A woman slid off the horse's rump and crumpled to the ground. The rider wheeled the horse around and galloped off in the direction he had come. The woman lay there a bit and then began trying to get up, using only her left arm. She made it to her feet and began walking slowly toward the house, while holding her right arm with her left. It was the little woman I had shot.

Brenda Ann and Toby held their positions and let her come. I knew they would be watching in all directions, alert to the possibility that the woman was intended to distract and expose us. True to my thoughts, I heard Cajun and Rusty on the attack up on the ridge east of Brenda Ann. There was a shot, and I listened carefully to hear both dogs. They were both still on the attack, so the shot at the dogs must have missed. I heard Brenda Ann stifling a laugh as the barking of the dogs went over the ridge.

There was a shot from the mule pasture, and I heard the bullet whine as it glanced off a rock near the barn. Toby's rifle answered. The woman kept coming, seemingly unmindful of the commotion. She was close enough now that I could see that her face was etched with pain.

This day was certainly not going as Brenda Ann and I had planned. By this time she was to be removing frames full of honey and brushing off the bees. I was to be uncapping the combs and spinning out the honey. Truly, we never know what a day will bring forth. How many times had I heard Ma and Pa say that, while reminding me to stay right with God?

Peggy Frances had been going from window to window and door to door. She had strapped on a holster with pistol, and she had Pa's old shotgun in her hand. "That woman's gonna be at the front steps, and she's wounded." I told her. "I shot her in the shoulder because she was drawing a bead on Brenda Ann. She really needs help, but I will bet she has a hideout pistol or knife, or both."

"If she wants my help, she will strip down to her skin. Brenda Ann and I can handle that." Peggy Frances had always been a no-nonsense kind of girl when things got serious. Cajun and Rusty were alongside the woman now. They were wary, but they knew she was wounded. They seemed to want to help.

"I'm hurt and I'm hurting like I never hurt before," she said at the foot of the steps. "This pain is terrible." The pain seemed to be taking her breath and making it difficult for her to talk. I was still watching from the window for any activity behind her, but I saw none.

I heard her say to Brenda Ann, "I tried to shoot you. Another second and I would have had you dead center. I hope you are a better person than I am. I need help." I heard Brenda Ann telling her she would help her up the steps as soon as she checked her for a knife or pistol.

"I've got both," she said. "With that bunch of men I run with, it's necessary. And there's a straight razor between my breasts."

They were soon in the house, and Brenda Ann put a derringer, a long thin knife and a straight razor on a high shelf. They steered her toward the back bedroom, and I swung on my crutches to the stove. Coals remained from breakfast, and very shortly I had a hot fire going. Soon a pot of water was boiling.

The woman was talking, talking as if she needed to get loads and loads of bad experiences and memories off her chest. "Nat was good to me, so I stuck with him even though I knew from the first that he was no good. He thinks that only fools work for a living, but we have lived like varmints, from one hole to another. My pa was pizen mean when he was drinking, and that was most of the time. Nat was good to me and told me that he was going to be somebody one day, so I ran off with him."

Peggy Frances poured off some of the boiling water into a pan so that it could cool. In a low voice she told me, "We are going to have to send for the doctor. I think the bones in her shoulder are messed up. The bullet went through, and the exit wound on the back of the shoulder looks pretty bad, but it's about quit bleeding." We both turned to listen to what she was saying to Brenda Ann.

"All they wanted to talk about for the last five days was what a good time they were going to have with you when they caught you. Bully was for killing you after a couple of weeks, but the others wanted to keep you around for four or five months. They kept talking about how pretty you are and how much woman you are. What made me so mad was that Nat was saying the same thing."

She stopped talking long enough to sob deep heart-rending sobs. "They told Nat he couldn't have a turn with you unless he let them take turns with me. And he was thinking of going along with that. That's why I hated you so much and wanted to kill you. I had the perfect excuse when you opened that gate to let the horses out."

Well, that answered the question of why I saw such hate in her face when she was taking aim on Brenda Ann. Thinking ahead, I knew they were going to try another attack on us. And soon. They were using her as bait to distract us. Now, they had to get her back or kill her because she knew too much about their operations.

Suddenly two rifle shots sounded down the hill in the direction of the Marlow residence. They were too close together to be from the same gun. Peggy Frances had said that her father could be expected at almost any time. Surely the earlier shots would have alerted him to be careful. Soon Mr. Marlow and Bobby Jack came riding into the yard, and we learned what had happened.

One of the outlaws stepped into the road in front of them as they were walking their horses and keeping a careful lookout. To Bobby Jack he said, "You skinny squirt, drop that rifle and then get off that hoss. Both of you. They're my hosses now. And old man, you jes' take it slow and easy with that bad arm."

Bobby Jack came off the horse with gun in hand, and he fired as he hit the ground. The would-be horse thief got his shot off first, but he had not brought the barrel down to Bobby Jack's crouched level. The shot went over his head, but Bobby Jack's shot went through the robber's head. "I warn't aimin' for his head," Bobby Jack said. "Fact is, I warn't aimin' at all. I was tryin' to shoot him in his chest. He was so close, not ten feet away."

"I don't like killin' a man," Bobby Jack added. "I got sick and vomited." He paused. "I will help dig the hole, but I don't want to help bury him. I don't want to look at him again."

From the bedroom, Sukey called out. That's what she said her name was, "Sukey." "What did he look like?"

Mr. Marlow answered her question. "Tall, real tall," he said. "Dark hair, and a bad scar above his left eye."

Sukey didn't answer for a little while, and then she said in a strange low voice. "Well, I'm a widow now. And I don't really care. At this time last week I would have sobbed and mourned, but he ruined all of that over the last few days."

Brenda Ann came out of the bedroom where Sukey lay on the bed. "We have done all we can for her. We need to send for the doctor as soon as we think it safe to send someone."

"It won't be safe for quite a while," I ventured. "They are apparently thinking that instead of trying to round up their horses, they will just try to grab horses wherever they can find them."

Toby had just come in from his post near the barn, and he was thinking the same thing. That was the main reason for taking a stand where he could watch the horses. He had not seen or heard anything suspicious, but that didn't really mean anything.

"Can I talk to Sukey? Is she covered?" I asked.

"Just a moment," answered Brenda Ann. After less than a minute she invited me into the bedroom. Sukey's face showed the physical pain she was feeling, but I saw something more. There was a grim resolve. This woman wasn't defeated, but what did she have in mind? I wished that I could read her thoughts.

"I'm sorry I shot you," I told her. "But you didn't give me any choice. I'm glad I didn't kill you, and I hope you make a full recovery."

"I figgered for a long time that I would wind up shot or stabbed, running with that bunch," she said. "It might as well have been you as somebody else."

"Will you tell me how many is in that bunch?" I asked. "There were nine horses."

"Ain't but three left now," she said, "since that boy killed Nat. One of 'em is Bully, the one you shot in the leg a couple months ago. You called him something else. Nat was the only one who would stand up to him. He's pure pizen. He will do anything. And I mean anything. I'm warning you."

She paused a bit, and I could tell that she was tensing her muscles against the pain. "He was the one who wanted to drop me off here to bait y'all out into the open and get you to drop your guard. I looked for Nat to call him on it, but he went along with it. I believe Nat was thinking about your Brenda Ann."

I couldn't help glancing toward Brenda Ann when she said "your Brenda Ann," but I couldn't read a thing in her face. Most women would have shown some kind of reaction to that.

Sukey echoed my thoughts in her next statement. "They'll be

71

trying to kill me. And it probably won't be long when they figger out that Nat is dead. I can tell a lot about where they sell horses and other stuff. And where they lay up between times. They know I hate them, and they wouldn't trust me if I went back to them."

She seemed to be turning something over in her mind. "And Bully hates you. I don't know why, but he hates you. That's why we were camped here. He was trying to find out where you were. Nat told him we needed to be moving on, and I think Nat would have had his way if all of them had not seen Brenda Ann."

After gritting her teeth against the pain, she continued. "They wanted that horse too, except for Nat. Nat told them that a fine horse like that would be known, that he wouldn't bring anything but trouble. Nat had better judgment about things than the others, except maybe Peewee. Peewee don't say much, and he comes across as sorta stupid. But he ain't stupid."

"Do you have any whiskey?" she asked. "I need some whiskey for this pain. I'm hurtin' bad."

Before I could answer, Mr. Marlow spoke from just outside the bedroom door. "I have about half of a bottle in my saddle bag, Rick. I was using it when my arm was hurting real bad. I don't use it otherwise."

He started out the front door to his horse, but before he stepped out on the porch Cajun and Rusty attacked something near his horse. A man's desperate voice pleaded, "Call them off! Call them off!"

Toby spoke to the dogs from the barn, and when I made it to the door, they were standing before a dirty little man with their teeth bared. Tatters of torn cloth exposed bloody

wounds from sharp teeth. He had enough sense to remain perfectly still.

"Move real slow and unbuckle that holster," Toby called. "Don't let it fall. Nothing that sudden. Lay it on the ground "

"I've been watching you snake down that hill, and I knew what was going to happen when those dogs scented you on the crosswind." Toby commented. "You are good, but those dogs don't have to hear you or see you."

"Don't step out into the yard, Mr. Marlow," Toby cautioned. "He's probably got somebody covering him up on the ridge. We will send Cajun and Rusty to check that out, and I will cover them."

Toby had no sooner spoken than his rifle spoke as well. "Missed him," Toby said. "I hurried the shot. He was taking aim on this little guy. He must know some things they don't want him to tell."

When the dogs started toward the top of the hill, I heard the distinct sound of running feet headed east. By the time the dogs reached the ridge, we heard the drum of hoof beats of a fast-moving horse. The rider was making sure that no one could overtake him.

"Sounds like y'all caught Peewee," I heard Sukey say. "He was the one who always stole the horses. He would crawl on his belly and make no sound at all. For some reason he never spooked the horses. They would do whatever he wanted them to do."

"He was gonna kill me," the little man said incredulously. "He was gonna kill me! After all I have done for him, Bully was gonna kill me."

I was thinking that if Sukey had told the truth, and I believed she had, then there were only two men out there now to

worry about. I needed to ask her about the one man now left with Bing. I wanted to know more about him.

I also wondered how Sukey would manage to support herself. Her man left a saddle, bridle, six-shooter and a rifle that rightly belonged to her now. He had enough money on him to buy a good horse and have some left. That thought reminded me that we needed to check their camp for any other saddles or other stuff. After all was said and done she might end up with one of the horses we turned loose.

"You are filthy." It was Bobby Jack. He was looking Peewee over. "How long has it been since you had a bath? You ain't much bigger'n I am."

I turned away so Bobby Jack wouldn't see me laughing. I looked at my bee colonies. According to Brenda Ann, the supers were brimming full of good quality honey. I wanted to start spinning it out. As I worked through the frames of honey I would watch for the point at which the bees had shifted from one nectar source to another, and I would avoid mixing the honey. That involved quite a bit of tasting, and I liked that.

Tomorrow would be second Sunday preaching service, and the outlaw activity would be the major topic of conversation as people stood around outside the church building. Hopefully, I would be able to start spinning honey Monday. My patience was wearing thin. I had endured the indoor confinement lying still on a bed. Now that I was moving around, albeit on crutches, I was impatient to get on with things.

As Brenda Ann had reported to me about the bee colonies, their importance to me grew in my mind. Wanting to gain a decent degree of financial independence, and wanting a life close to nature in the beautiful Ozarks, the bees afforded the best opportunity I could see. And Brenda Ann loved to work with them! I couldn't believe my good luck.

At that thought, something seemed to prod me somewhere deep inside. Luck? Was it luck? Or was The One above looking out for me in a very special way? And what obligations did that place on me? Brenda Ann had told me that I should not take anything for granted. What did she mean by that? Suddenly it seemed that there was no way I could live life without her.

PROGRESS

I gained immense satisfaction from seeing the honey flow out of the combs into the bottom of the vat. The lighter colored and usually milder flavored honey came first; there were several different flavors among the frames of lighter colored honey. Some I could not identify as to source. My favorite was honey from holly nectar, and I had many customers who asked for holly honey. Although lighter in color, it has a strong taste that a person either likes very much or dislikes. It is not a neutral flavor.

Turning the handle to spin out the honey taxed my strength, but helped rebuild it. I had lost much strength and stamina while lying in bed. Brenda Ann worked hard and long in the July heat. Although we were both tired at the end of the day, we enjoyed our ride back to the Scroggins place. We remained alert to bushwhackers, mindful that Bing Hodges and the other man of the gang remained at large. There might be others not affiliated with them.

The way Sukey described the raw lust and the willingness to kill that ran through the gang when they saw Brenda Ann, made me do some thinking. I know how men can go crazy over a pretty woman, and most men will put their own lives at risk to protect a woman. The willingness to abuse and then to kill a woman was something I had never encountered or thought about. It reminded me that when men cross the line into wrongdoing, there are no clear limits to their evil.

We now trusted Sukey with the weapons she carried on her person when she came to us. We all expected Bing to make an effort to kill her, and she might need them. The doctor rigged a sort of harness to immobilize her shoulder while she carried her right arm in a sling. Although she was right-handed, she used her left well enough to be a lot of help around the place. I noticed that when she was outside, she was as alert as a deer to every sound and movement.

Her upbringing by an abusive father and an abused mother mired in the worst kind of poverty, together with her life with an outlaw, made her rough and ready. But she had a kind streak that ran broad and deep, whether it was directed toward a person or animal. Sukey took a special liking to Bobby Jack, and he to her. They both spoke their minds in clear terms. Sometimes starkly clear.

The sheriff took Peewee into custody, but the only charge that he could bring against him was attempted horse theft for his failed effort to steal Mr. Marlow's horse. I suppose Peewee could have claimed that he was bellying down the hill for some other reason, but he freely admitted that his intent was to steal Mr. Marlow's horse.

After talking with Sukey about Peewee, and after having a long talk with Peewee himself, Mr. Marlow decided that instead of pressing charges against him, he would offer him a job. Sukey knew Peewee from almost two years of experience to be a devoted follower. He lived by a simple unwritten code, and when he accepted a man as his leader, he gave that man his complete loyalty. He spoke occasionally of Bully's effort to kill him, a betrayal that shook him to his core.

Mr. Marlow cleaned out a corner of the tack and harness room for his living quarters. Peewee possessed an uncanny understanding and affection for horses and mules. He loved being around them, and they welcomed his presence. At Bobby Jack's insistence, Peewee began to take regular baths, and I wondered if his newfound cleanliness might affect the way the horses felt about him. It did nothing to harm his way with the horses and mules, but it did a great deal to improve his relationship with people.

He took over all the basic care of the Marlow horses and mules, which included four new mules almost as big as the doctor's mule. One of them was a real problem to handle, but it wasn't long until Peewee had him settled down and pulling the freight wagon as if he really enjoyed it. The freight-line to Springfield got off to a good start, but Mr. Marlow said that he knew the railroad would put them out of business sooner or later.

My two sisters came back with the wagons on one of the trips. Each summer they spent a few weeks visiting with me and maintaining their ties with the homeplace. They shared their old bedroom with one another, and the house once again had five people in it for the first time since Ma and Pa were living. I could tell that Lou Evelyn just enjoyed being back in the Ozark countryside, but Betty Jean seemed to have something weighing on her mind.

After a week or so I found an opportunity to ask her about what seemed to be bothering her. It took some coaxing, but finally she asked if I would consider buying her one-third interest in the place we had inherited. She explained that she and her slick-talking friend were talking of marriage, and he wanted to start a business.

"Well Betty Jean," I said, "I had planned to ask you and Lou Evelyn at some point if you wanted to sell. I get the feeling that Lou Evelyn may want to keep her third and have it divided out to her. I couldn't pay you all at one time unless I could get someone to loan me the money. Could you let me pay you over a two or three year period?"

I was going to have a hard time thinking of Harland as a brother-in-law. That was his name. "Harland." She seemed to sort of squirm a bit when I mentioned paying her in two or three annual installments.

"Well, Harland needs all the money at one time to get the business started," she said. She ducked her head and looked at her feet when she told me that, like she was ashamed to say it. When I asked her what kind of business, she seemed even more self-conscious.

We were standing in the shade of a huge elm near the largest group of the bee hives, and the bees were going and coming near us in the early morning sun. In spite of the dry weather, they were still finding plenty of nectar and pollen. I might get to take off a little fall honey, although it would not be as good quality. I erred on the side of caution when it came to gathering fall honey. One never knew how tough the winter might be, how late the spring might be, and how much honey the bees would need to carry them through in good condition.

As Betty Jean hesitated before answering my question about the nature of the proposed business venture, I could see genuine pain in her face. "Well, he said he wanted to play his cards close to his chest, and he didn't want to take a chance on me inadvertently dropping a clue to what he had in mind. It's some kind of investment business. That's all he would say. He said that it's such a promising opportunity that others will jump in ahead of him if they get wind of it."

I was only nineteen, but having to make my own way since I was twelve had given me a measure of understanding that made me feel more comfortable among people who were ten to twenty years older than among those my own age. My sister was about to be taken for a ride, a ride that would shake her faith in everyone, even in God above. The words I spoke were chosen carefully. She would jump to defend the chiseler if I spoke my mind.

"Well, Sis," I said, "One of the last things Pa told me was that I should remember that you and Lou Evelyn share in the place. He also made me promise to look out for the two of you concerning any business deal. You know I've been mindful to honor Ma and Pa by living up to the confidence they placed in me. Do you see the spot this puts me in?"

She looked down at the ground and nodded her head. She played with a little rock with the toe of her shoe. "Harland said he would give me two weeks to get your agreement, and then he's coming to visit for a couple of days."

She played with the stone some more. The next words seemed to come hard. "He said that if you wouldn't buy at a good price, he could find an investor who would buy my part from me. He said that he knew a man who was looking to buy a place in these parts."

I could feel myself getting upset, and I decided I had better end the conversation for now. "Let's do this, Betty Jean. Let us both think about it and pray about it for two or three days. You may remember Pa saying that anything too hot to sleep on just might be too hot to handle."

She seemed relieved, at least temporarily. I had tried to accept the idea of having a brother-in-law that didn't measure up to family standards, but now I knew that I had to find a way to shake her loose from this underhanded swindler. I thought of Sukey and of the years of misery she had spent with a man who figured to get along without working.

I needed to talk to a lawyer, but it would be hard now to find time to go see one. I wished I could talk to Mr. Scroggins. What little I knew, I didn't believe Betty Jean could sell without Aunt Carrie's consent. And Aunt Carrie was not likely to okay a sale until she was absolutely sure that the money would benefit Betty Jean.

On the other hand, when she turned eighteen, Betty Jean could get married without Aunt Carrie's consent, and then Harland would have the say-so on the sale. I had a feeling that Aunt Carrie didn't have any better opinion of Harland than I did. I would find a chance to sound out Lou Evelyn. She could surely shed some light on the situation.

We started back to the house. Brenda Ann had supers of combs ready for me to uncap and to spin the honey out. I was managing the crutches much better now, and I was putting a little weight on my right foot without it aching and hurting. My strength was coming back fast, but it had a long way to go.

A couple of days had passed, and I had not yet talked with Lou Evelyn. I had done a great deal of talking with the Good Lord. As if in answer to the prayers, Bobby Jack came with some jaw-dropping news for Betty Jean. He had ridden with Peewee and his dad to Springfield. While Mr. Marlow was inside the shipping office, he and Peewee waited outside. Suddenly, Peewee disappeared.

Looking for Peewee, he walked around a corner and saw Harland counting out some money to a large burly man he didn't know, a man with a bad scar down the right jaw and across his chin. When he later found Peewee, he learned that Peewee ducked out of sight of the same man. He knew that man as "Bully."

We all looked at Betty Jean. The color had drained from her face. "Well that doesn't mean anything," she protested. "I'm sure Harland can give a good explanation for that."

I'm thinking that we all had the same silent response. "Yeah, I'm sure he can." Even though none of us spoke that thought out loud, Betty Jean knew that we were thinking it.

I knew better than to push it. She felt obligated to defend not only him, but also her choice in men. She would have to spend some time alone, mulling the information that had come to her from a young lad who could sometimes be brutally honest. In her quiet times she would weigh that against all the other things she knew about Harland. I had to trust that her intelligence and common sense would win out. More than that, I had to trust God to work it out.

But Sukey couldn't hold her tongue. "Child, I hope you don't mess up like I did. I married a silver-tongued scoundrel. But I had a better excuse than you do. I was gettin' away from a mean drunk daddy."

I changed the subject. "You and Peewee have become real good friends, Bobby Jack. Peewee is an interesting man. He really has a way with horses and mules."

"He would rather be around them than with people!" Bobby Jack declared emphatically. Bobby Jack absolutely loved to be with people, and he found Peewee's pronounced preference for equine company to be amazing.

"He don't sleep on his cot in the harness room. He puts his bedroll in the feed trough, and that's where he sleeps so he can be close to the mules." I was thinking that there was probably a lot more to it than that. He didn't want to get trapped in a room. The mule barn had a back door and two side doors. The split log trough afforded some protection from flying lead, and the mules would likely alert him to an intruder.

"I'm thinking that he believes Bing Hodges, 'Bully,' will come after him sooner or later," I told Bobby Jack. "He probably figures he stands a better chance if he is in the feed trough." I thought it well that Bobby Jack and Mr. Marlow be thinking along those same lines.

"I thought about that, too," Bobby Jack replied. "A lot of people think Peewee is stupid. He ain't stupid. He jus' don't talk much. When I got him to talkin', I found out he knows all kinds of stuff, and he can figger out things."

When Brenda Ann and I were saddling up for the return trip, I noticed Lou Evelyn and Betty Jean in earnest conversation at the foot of the front steps. I saw Betty Jean wipe her cheeks with her hand and then wipe her hand on her apron. Facing the truth can be tough, sometimes devastating.

Riding alert to danger, Brenda Ann and I had virtually memorized the location and appearance of every tree and rock between my place and the Scroggins house. Sometimes we would rein in the horses and talk about changes in the landscape, for it changed slightly every day. Patches of weeds that had grown up over the past month offered new places of concealment. Bushes grew wider and thicker.

We also talked about how we both loved the land with its variety of trees, birds and four-footed animals. We saw a roadrunner occasionally, and on our morning trip we sometimes heard his dovelike call. It was the only one I had seen in the county. Their regular habitat lay farther west. The Cardinals also sang melodious series of tweets. A hawk sometimes dipped to the ground to claim a meal. I always had to worry about them claiming my young chickens.

On this afternoon I began to think of the changing situation. Good progress was being made, but Brenda Ann had put her future on hold to help me as only she could. Was I to be in her future? Was she investing in her future by helping me, or was it all just a remarkable act of goodwill? She had told me not to take anything for granted, but she had suggested that I might ask her to marry me. Or had she? It was not clear.

Toby was making good progress on the new house for him and his bride. He had already mentioned that my leg would be fully mended at just about the time they would be moving into their new home. Peggy Frances had asked me about moving some of the hens and a young rooster with them. I had many more than I needed, but that turned out to be a good thing with all the extra mouths to feed during this summer. We had greatly reduced the number of young roosters by converting them to fried chicken on the dining table.

A widower with two half-grown children was showing an interest in Sukey at church, and he called on her a couple of times at my home. He was a good solid man, a good provider for his family, and I could see the two of them making a good match if he could adjust to her plain-spoken ways. He seemed to like that about her. She made him laugh, something he had done very little since his wife had died almost two years earlier.

Although I had lived alone for seven years, the past months with the Scroggins family had me feeling differently about resuming my former existence. There had been a constant stream of Scroggins progeny in and out of the house, and never a time when at least two or three of Brenda Ann's relatives were not there. Like Mr. and Mrs. Scroggins, they were good-natured but serious people, and they all shared a love of The Ozarks.

Brenda Ann had not shared with me what she had in mind for the fall and winter months. She had mentioned her intention to help me market my honey in Springfield. She had talked a little about how she had helped her father in his business office, but she indicated no desire to return to that. I had been content to focus my entire attention on the matters immediately at hand, and there were certainly enough of those to keep my mind busy. The realization that I must start thinking ahead jolted me.

The Scroggins place was beginning to feel like home, and Brenda Ann's family felt like family to me. And she and I talked about things almost like a man and wife. Even so, she had a reserve that I did not try to penetrate. She kept me wondering about how she might feel toward me as her mate in life. Perhaps that was because I had my own reservations that I did not share with her.

Like Mr. and Mrs. Scroggins, all the Scroggins offspring loved The Ozarks, but they soon went scurrying back to the city. Was that the way it would be with Brenda Ann? Was she just helping an old friend during the summer, only to gladly head back to the city in the fall? After all, winters in The Ozarks, although usually mild and enjoyable, could sometimes get tough.

Toby and Peggy Frances, like Brenda Ann, had proven to be friends of the rarest sort, and I had no idea what I would have done without them. Their marriage had gotten off to an abrupt and busy start. I could sense their excitement at the prospect of moving into their new home. Toby's blacksmithing business had done quite well over the summer, giving them some extra cash to work with.

I learned after we had unsaddled, fed and watered the horses that Brenda Ann had been doing some thinking of her own. "I have to make plans, Rick, for the months ahead, and I'm not sure what I want to do. You won't really need me any-more, but I don't feel any desire to go back to the city. I guess I have become a bona fide country girl."

My heart jumped and then skipped a beat. Again, the words just came out of my mouth of their own volition. I'm not in the habit of speaking without thinking first, except, that is, when I'm talking to Brenda Ann. "I need you, Brenda Ann, in ways that have nothing to do with bee hives. I can't imag-ine ever not needing you."

She looked at me with just a slight grin, but I could see that her eyes were dancing with a new light. "If that's a proposal, Rick, that's not the way to do it. But I'm most pleased to hear you say that. We won't talk about it anymore right now. We can get back to it later." She strode ahead of me toward the house as I came swinging along at a much slower pace on my crutches.

STEADY BUT READY

Lou Evelyn often found herself in the role of cautioning and steadying her older sister, almost as if there was a role reversal and she was the older sister. Of course, there was only little more than a year's difference in their ages. It was just that Betty Jean got more excited over the "knight-in-shining-armor" and "prince-and-princess" type scenarios. Lou Evelyn had a firmer grip on reality, and found enough satisfaction in real life situations that she felt little need to enhance them with her imagination.

She had bitten her tongue numerous times when Betty Jean talked in excited tones about what Harland planned for the two of them. Betty Jean accused her of being jealous when she spoke words of caution and skepticism. Aunt Carrie, likewise, tried to bring her to a more realistic view. It seemed that their efforts were counter-productive, and they both learned that silence was better. Then she accused them of failing to support her in her happiness.

The very credible words from Bobby Jack had shaken Betty Jean to her core, largely because she had already begun to have her own doubts about Harland. He had failed to make good on several smaller promises he had made to her, promises that were unsolicited and unnecessary. His vagueness as to his business activities, as well as to his plans for the future, had begun to bother her. Women like details, and she was no different from other women in that regard.

Even so, she surprised Lou Evelyn when she sought Lou Evelyn's thoughts and opinion after she heard Bobby Jack's story. "I have begun to distrust my woman's intuition," she told her younger sister in an uncertain and anxious voice. "I don't have confidence in my own ability to make vital decisions. I need you to help me get my head straight, Lou Evelyn."

She continued. "You never seem to have any problem making up your mind about things, and you can see when something is not all it's claimed to be. Like when you sent Slim Wofford on his way. Boy, was he good looking! Had money to spend. But you just knew that underneath those winning ways, he was a crook. And now he's locked up, along with those other big-talking guys."

"What do you think, Lou Evelyn? Couldn't there be a good reason Harland was paying Bing Hodges some money? I mean, even if Bing Hodges is a crook, Harland might not know that. If he had something to sell and it was a good buy, Harland might just be making a good investment."

Lou Evelyn knew she had to answer carefully. She saw the crack in her sister's stubborn refusal to see Harland as he really was, but if she pushed it too hard, Betty Jean might just go back to defending him. She knew that her sister had invested a lot of emotion in her hopes of a glowing future with Harland, and she might not be willing to give up on those hopes.

"Betty Jean, you don't make your decision based on that situation alone, even as incriminating as it appears. If you think back, I believe you will think of other explanations Harland made that were short on details. He just expected you to take his word when you wanted a more complete explanation." Lou Evelyn was recalling several instances when she had overheard conversations between the two of them.

Tears began to flow down Betty Jean's cheeks as she recalled the doubts she had at other times, doubts she had brushed aside in favor of the idyllic future that she suddenly realized existed only in her imagination. She wiped the tears from her cheeks and dried her hand on her apron. It was hard, so hard, to give up on Harland.

She wondered what Lou Evelyn would think if she knew about Harland pressuring her to raise money for him by selling her one-third interest in their inheritance. No, she didn't wonder. She knew exactly what she would think. And Lou Evelyn would have no difficulty in telling a paramour "No" if he suggested selling her inheritance to finance a business scheme scarce on details.

"Big sister, I have been doing some thinking since we got here," Lou Evelyn said. They both watched their brother spring onto Dan's back with only one good leg to spring with. "Rick is largely the man he is because he has managed for himself here among these rocks, trees and streams. And I have been looking at other men who have grown up here on the land. I have made a definite decision. This is where I'm going to find my husband."

"Look at Toby. I know there are good men in Springfield, but how long would you have to look to find one who is Toby's match for maturity and responsibility? I love this land, and I like the men who love it." Her words caught Betty Jean's interest. She had wondered why Lou Evelyn showed no more interest in young men. She had concluded that she was just developing slowly along those lines, although she had certainly developed physically.

"Think about it Betty Jean. When Toby brought Sam and Barney to eat supper with us after they finished a long day's work on the new house, they were hot, dirty and sweaty, but they were good company. They washed up outside and came in real polite and thankful for a good meal. Their hands are rough, and their faces are brown, but they are men, real men. And they had just finished a full day of honest work and real accomplishment."

Betty Jean, caught up in the character analysis, added her thoughts. "Yes, it wasn't hard to see their satisfaction as they talked about what they had done that day and what they would be doing the next day. As tired as they must have been, it was like they were looking forward to getting up before daylight to be there at daybreak the next morning."

"Yeah, at this time of year the more a body can do before the sun gets up in the sky, the better. Betty Jean, I want to find me a man like one of them. You hear people talking about matching mules or horses in a team. I feel sorry for a hard-pulling mule that is paired with one that won't pull his share of the load. You won't ever have to worry about a man like Sam or Barney doing his part."

Betty Jean smiled, and Lou Evelyn thought that was a good thing to see. Betty Jean didn't smile much anymore. She looked at Lou Evelyn teasingly. "I believe Barney was a bit taken by you. He kept looking at you when you were look-ing in another direction." Lou Evelyn could feel the blood rushing to her cheeks.

In the meanwhile, Bing Hodges had worked his way back into the area, together with another man and a pack horse. He had begun to use the name "Johnny Jones" when he per-mitted himself to be seen in a public place. He cursed "that Weber kid" every time his hand strayed to the rough scar on his right jaw and chin. That rock-scarred horseshoe had really messed up his face, and sooner or later that kid was going to pay with his life.

As much as he didn't like to admit it to himself, that "kid" had grown into an impressive man. Everything he knew about him told him that Weber was a good man to leave alone. Even at age fourteen, he had not shrunk back as he had expected, but he met him with teeth bared. He retreated only to gain room to maneuver and strike back. Now he was five years older and in prime manhood. The thought sent a chill through him.

He had prided himself on being able to change his appearance as he changed his name. That ability had served him well and enabled him to avoid apprehension on several occasions. Now, even a full growth of beard would not cover the scar. It extended wide and long down his jawline and across his chin, and no whiskers grew on it.

The man riding with him was a lean and intense man with restless eyes. He gave the impression of being constantly aware of all around him. A bit taller than Bing, he weighed thirty pounds less. Somehow he immediately conveyed the message that he was much more interested in listening and looking than talking.

If Bing's operation continued to work as anticipated for another year, he would drift to California and make up a nice yarn as to how he got the scar. He would have enough money to buy a nice place out in the countryside and become a respected man in the community. If this new guy, Harland, kept coming through for him, he might make it even sooner.

What a stroke of luck when he learned that Harland was dating Weber's sister, and he also didn't like Weber. That kid had been bad luck from the first. Who would have thought that a twelve-year old could be that savvy and rear up on his hind feet the way he did when they went to get him. While the deputy was trying to slip up on him, it was him, Bing, who he was eyeing, even though he well knew what the deputy was doing.

And then he turned the tables on him as quick as a wink when he was just fourteen. Although he resisted the thought, he was afraid to go anywhere near Weber. Something always went wrong. He had another bad scar just healed from the last time he tried to get him. In fact his leg still bothered him some from that gunshot wound.

The kid had a weakness, though. He was soft-hearted. It's a tough world and a soft heart just won't cut it. In fact, in Bing's mind a soft heart was downright dangerous. Like when Weber let him walk this past spring when he could have finished him off. Now that he had let him live, he was going to get that soft-hearted fool. That, in his mind, proved him right and Weber wrong.

Those cursed dogs of his! Whatever plan he came up with, he had to think about them. He had spent hours running different plans through his mind, but those dogs always proved to be the defect in his plans. Except for them, he could find a good sniper spot and take him out with one well-placed shot. He could be very patient in an ambush and he was a good shot with a rifle, one of the best. But with his luck where Weber was concerned, those dogs would flush him out for sure.

He had already tried poisoning the dogs, but they wouldn't take the bait. He couldn't understand that. That big dog; he was a monster. He had never seen a dog like that before. Where had the kid gotten him? He looked like he might be part wolf.

Now Harland said he would handle the job! And he would do it with pleasure! It would be well worth the haul they would make on this trip to get him to take care of the job. He needed to find out Harland's last name and a few more things about him. He felt uncomfortable that he didn't know more about him. Information can be power.

Harland would be able to get close to Weber without being suspected of anything. He said he could do it and make it look like someone else had done it, or even make it look like an accident. And for him, the dogs would not be a problem. He had jumped at the chance to get a load without having to pay for it.

That part posed a problem with his partner. He would not like killing Weber, and he certainly would not be willing to part with his share of the loot to get it done. He was playing with two or three stories to explain the nonpayment. He would settle on one of them when the time arrived.

Harland's apparent eagerness at being able to get a load in exchange for taking out his potential brother-in-law had sparked suspicion in Bing. Harland had assured him that the money would always be ready when he delivered his payload, but on the last delivery, he had muttered something about getting a lot of money tied up. Their agreement was that the jewelry and other goods would not be resold for at least a year and that the sales would happen outside Missouri, preferably several states away.

If Harland was running tight on money, he might sell sooner and closer, and Bing well knew that was the way most burglars got caught. Stolen goods had a way of being traced back to the burglar. His employment by the Robinsons had gotten him into the homes of some very affluent people, almost all of whom had safes. He had waited for years for Yancey to get out of the big house.

He would have been in the big house with him except for his ability to assume a new identity. Yancey had been loyal and did not squeal on him. He and Yancey shared the same mother, a tall pretty woman with an eye for a quick buck. Yancey's father was an older man, and his mother lived high on his money. He died under mysterious circumstances, and she continued to live high on his money until it was all gone.

Only she knew who sired Bing, if even she knew. She died in a saloon brawl when Bing was seventeen years old, and Bing went to live with Yancey. Yancey earned a steady but modest income as a locksmith's apprentice. Bing poked fun at him for not using his knowledge to get some real money. He complained because Yancey would not dole out spending money to him as his mother had.

Tiring of the complaints and ridicule, and seeing some tempting opportunities to put his hands on some sizable sums of money, he succumbed to temptation. He had a special interest in safes, and he studied all kinds until his knowledge of them exceeded that of Mr. Carson, his employer. A cautious man by nature, he painstakingly planned his thefts with the utmost care. Many safes he could open without damaging the safe.

Opening a safe without having to damage the safe offered many advantages, the main one being that it deflected suspicion. The first suspects were those who had the safe's combination or could contrive to get it. His ability to pick locks enabled him to enter and leave the premises without leaving any evidence of unauthorized entry.

Since his release from prison, Yancey had made it a point to stay out of public view. Before and at the time of his release from prison, he dropped the word that he was going to New Orleans to live with his sister. He didn't have a sister, but no one knew that, and that was all the better. When he dropped out of sight, they would be less likely to question his absence. Because he didn't have a sister, any efforts to find him through her would be futile. And when a series of safes were burglarized, they would surely try to find him.

Actually, that idea came from Bing. He even produced a woman claiming to be his sister to visit him at the prison. Bing was good at that kind of thing, and that talent was one of the few things in his life that came honest. He inherited it from their mother. She would deceive people just for the fun of manipulating them. It made her feel superior to her victims.

Shortly after Yancey went to prison, Bing assumed his identity of "Bing Hodges" and found the first gainful employment of his life with the Robinsons. While Yancey was living the tough life of a prisoner, he was living the good life with Mrs. Robinson. She was the trophy wife of her much older husband, and she soon made it clear to Bing that he could be much more to her than a hired man. Mr. Robinson often went out of town without his wife, and Bing thoroughly enjoyed those times with her.

Like his mother, the cheating made him feel superior to Mr. Robinson. Robinson talked down to Bing quite often, or at least that was the way Bing took it. When that happened, Bing would think of his privileges with his employer's wife. That seemed to even things up. The fact that their liaisons were secret made him feel superior to the man who gave him orders. But when the time was right, he would reveal it to Robinson and laugh at him.

If it was possible for Bing to feel affection for anyone, he began to feel genuine affection for Mrs. Robinson. When she showed her loathing of him after the episode with Rick and Dan, he was hurt and embittered. When Mr. Robinson fired him, he felt sure she was behind it, but he blamed Rick and the scar on his face.

He had not told Yancey of his plans to go to California. Although Yancey had been loyal to him and saved him from a long prison stretch, Bing would ditch him when he had the money to go to California. Yancey's presence might lead to the discovery of his true identity. He would assume a new identity and not even Yancey would be able to find him.

There was one other thing that bothered him: Peewee! On the one hand, Peewee was slow mentally, or so it seemed, but on the other he seemed to intuitively know things that no one else knew. Peewee knew that he had tried to kill him, and he would not forget that. He needed to find a way to get rid of Peewee.

Peewee had been a handy and convenient tool, especially when the primary source of income was stolen horses. He had done Peewee a favor, and Peewee never forgot it when someone was nice to him. A pair of larger men were tormenting him, pushing and knocking him around and laughing at him for their own amusement. Bing decided to amuse himself by knocking them around.

He had a woman with him, and she pointed out to him how horrible it was to see a little guy tormented that way. "Somebody needs to do something to stop it," she said. Oh, it made him a big hero in her eyes when he dispatched them with ease. After knocking each of them down with his fists, he pulled them one by one to their feet and sent each of them on the way with a swift kick to the seat of the pants.

The woman began to fuss over Peewee, and he helped her see to it that he got a bath and some treatment for his cuts and bruises. Then he offered Peewee a job after Peewee told him that he made his living caring for horses and mules. He turned out to be a better hand than he could have imagined. And he was loyal, completely loyal.

There were three men in his horse-stealing group, and none of the three wanted to spend time shoeing and currying either the horses they rode or the ones they stole. Their laziness cost them money when they sold the horses, and they had even had to abandon horses that became lame because of their negligence. Ozark rocks were hard on the feet of horses.

Peewee expressed strong reluctance to steal horses, but the three of them persuaded him that it was a tough world where nobody really kept the rules, especially the ones who owned good horses. Then they discovered that he had the uncanny ability to get even the shyest of horses to go along with him. Their income greatly increased as the result of his talent and work.

Bing was glad to be out of the horse-stealing business. There was too much work, and the risks had steadily increased. With Yancey, he could make many times more money with less risk. Baldy, the only man that was left after he lost Nat and Peewee, decided to get out of the Ozark country and go west. He knew their failed attempt to capture a woman would rile up decent folks throughout the area.

Bing and Yancey kept themselves out of the public eye, and that meant traveling many of the same trails and using many of the same campsites that the gang had traveled with Peewee. Peewee might never talk, but Peewee knew that he was drawing down on him when that shot skinned tree bark just above Bing's head. He had to discard a good hat because the crown had a bullet hole in it. That was close.

He would be paying through the nose to get Weber disposed of, but it was worth it. That kid, now a full grown man, had been bad luck from the first. He would have to figure a way to get rid of Peewee without any help from anyone else. After all, he had done it before. It wouldn't be easy because Peewee seemed to know everything that was going on around him all the time. He would have to sneak up on him while he slept, and that wouldn't be easy either. He was a light sleeper.

Before Baldy pulled out, he had gone into town to get a feel for people's attitudes, and he came back ready to make tracks leading out of the country. He told Bing that Peewee was working for Marlow, and that he was sleeping in the harness room. Bing planned to kill him quietly while he slept without waking the Marlow family. Peewee was the best he had ever seen at moving quietly, but he was no slouch at that himself.

Ordinarily, he would scout the place in daylight, but he feared that Peewee would pick up on his presence. He would move on a moonlight night about midnight. That's when Peewee would be sleeping the soundest, and there would be several hours before his body was discovered. He would be well out of the area by that time.

He had to come up with a good excuse to get away from Yancey in order to do the job. Yancey had no patience with his grudges and hated any kind of violence. He had never carried a pistol, even before he went to prison. Yancey knew that an altercation his brother had at a saloon served to draw attention to the two of them before Yancey went to prison. In looking for Bing, they found Yancey and the loot from a recently opened safe.

With his ability to disguise himself and assume a new identity, Bing managed to slip through the dragnet that was set to capture him. He visited Yancey in prison in the guise of an old crippled uncle checking on his nephew. Now, he was the front man because Yancey couldn't show his face in public. That gave Bing the opportunity to lie to his older brother about the terms of the deal with Harland.

Meanwhile, Peewee knew more about Bing's whereabouts than Bing could imagine. As he and Bobby Jack were on their way to pick up some freight for Mr. Marlow, Peewee stopped the wagon. He got down and examined some hoof prints. "That's Bully's horse," he told Bobby Jack as he pointed to one set of tracks. He pointed to the tracks of another horse that had run alongside Bully's horse. "I ain't never seen them tracks."

"How long do you think it's been since they came along here?" Bobby Jack asked.

Peewee didn't hesitate. "About sunup this morning."

He stood still for long moments, and then he pulled his pistol from the holster. He rotated the chamber and made sure it was free of any grit that might interfere with its operation. Bobby Jack asked no more questions and made no further comment. He just studied Peewee much like he would a new horse. He found Peewee to be one of the most interesting people he had ever met, and Bobby Jack liked people.

A special bond marked the relationship between Bobby Jack and Peewee. As usual, Bobby Jack spoke his mind to Peewee in plain language, and Peewee listened. He made sure that Peewee bathed regularly and wore newly washed clothes. He got Claude, his older brother, to keep Peewee's hair trimmed.

Peewee talked more to Bobby Jack than he had talked to anyone in his entire life. He was full of interesting observations together with conclusions drawn from those observations. Bobby Jack was getting an education from him that he couldn't get anywhere else. Peewee instinctively knew what horses and mules liked and disliked and why. Moreover, he could explain why they reacted the way they did.

When he found Bobby Jack interested in what he had to say, it gave him a satisfaction he had never before experienced. No one had ever been interested in his thoughts and comments, and that led to his habitual silence. Raised by a widowed grandmother after his mother had died in childbirth, he had never known a father. His grandmother, a very small woman, was fiercely independent. She refused help from anyone, and she taught Peewee to never look to anyone else for help.

His grandmother died when he was fifteen, and he simply kept doing what he had already been doing to provide for the two of them. He helped neighbors with their horses and mules. Because he was dirty and unkempt and smelled of the barnyard, he became an object of ridicule. They paid him whatever amount they felt inclined for his work, and that was often much less than what was fair.

Bobby Jack learned that Peewee inherited his grandmother's small farm to which he intended to return. Before her death, she had cautioned him to always keep the property taxes paid, and he had faithfully followed her advice. With decent clothes and hygiene, he found himself increasingly accepted as one of the members of the community. He had even begun to attend church, a completely new experience for him.

He discovered a love for music he never knew he had. In his unfortunate life, he had heard music only a very few times, and he always had pressing concerns that distracted his attention from it. He formed the ambition to acquire a fiddle, an ambition he shared with Bobby Jack. He watched the dancers move their feet to the lively fiddle music---they called it clogging---and privately he ran the music through his mind while trying his own steps.

The gospel music was what really stirred his soul. They sang and preached about a man called "Jesus," and he wanted to find out more about that man. His grandmother had taught him numbers and the letters of the alphabet. He could write his name and read a few simple words. He wanted to learn to read. If he could read The Bible, it would tell him about Jesus.

He didn't want to kill a man. He had been with the gang when Bully killed a man, and he didn't ever want to see anything like that again. He knew though that he might have to kill Bully to keep from being killed. He was wondering whether to go after Bully before Bully came to him. He knew the places he would be more likely to find him.

Peewee's small farm, from the very first, became a favorite place to camp for Bully although he did not know it belonged to Peewee. Peewee guided the gang there at a time when the law was in hot pursuit. He knew how he could hide their trail and quietly lay up until the pursuers exhausted their efforts. Peewee made up his mind to ask for a short break from his work to check out his farm. At least for now, he would avoid any other campsites because he didn't want anyone to mistakenly associate him with Bully anymore.

He had already told Bobby Jack about the farm, and he would be honest with Mr. Marlow about his reason for asking for time off. Marlow would be surprised when he learned that Peewee owned some land. They didn't really need him on the upcoming freight run to Springfield, and this would be a good time for Mr. Marlow to let him off for a few days.

Marlow and his partner were always mindful of being ambushed by outlaws, and they had learned to value Peewee's keen sense of his surroundings on those freight runs. When Peewee asked to be excused from the upcoming trip, Marlow was reluctant to consent. The request reminded him of how valuable Peewee had become in just a short time.

"I will tell you what, Peewee. If you will go with us on this run, Bobby Jack and I will ride over there with you. I would sorta like to see your place, if you don't mind. A place ought not just be setting idle. I might work up some sort of business plan with you to put it to work."

Peewee showed his surprise. "Never thought about anything like that," he answered. "Just thought that one of these days I might build me a little house on it and move back there. The old one is leaking and rotten."

Bing had no idea Peewee was riding along on the trips to Springfield, and he made his move while Peewee was gone. Bobby Jack stayed home from that trip, and the next morning he saw Bing's tracks in the barnyard leading into the harness room. He immediately surmised that the man Peewee knew as "Bully" had made a futile effort to kill him. He set a wooden tub over a spot where there were several tracks close together so that they would be preserved.

His older brother, Claude, read sign pretty good, and the two of them were able to find where Bing had tied his horse. He remembered the tracks Peewee had identified as having been made by "Bully's" horse, and he remembered enough to know that these were the same. They decided to discuss the situation with their brother-in-law, Toby.

In the meanwhile, Bing's frustration was making him reckless. He told Yancey that he would be back to their camp by nightfall, and he knew that Yancey would move the camp before morning if he didn't show. Yancey was careful, and he wouldn't risk waiting in a fixed location if something had gone wrong.

Although Bing had no idea that Peewee owned any land at all, they were camped in the middle of his old home-place. The camp was only a few miles west of the route the freight wagons traveled to Springfield. He calculated that he could set up an ambush and still make it back to camp shortly after nightfall. His examination of tracks at daybreak told him that the wagons had been gone several days. Maybe this was the day they would make it back.

He had long dismissed the idea of a sniper shot because he knew how well Peewee could pick up on anything suspicious. Peewee had saved the gang from difficult circumstances several times because he saw or heard things of which no one else was aware. Bing's impatience and loss of sleep over-rode his sense of caution.

Peewee was handling the reins of the second wagon. He was dressed so neatly that Bing didn't recognize him at first. Peewee had always worn an old dirty cap, but now he had a new brown felt hat. A surge of irritation ranged through his body at the thought that the simple little man was holding a good job and prospering. That unkind thought prompted him to grunt and jerk his right fist upward.

That quick movement was enough to catch Peewee's eye. Bing saw a rifle suddenly appear in Peewee's right hand as his left hand wound the reins around a peg on his left. He recognized his voice as he yelled something to the other wagon. It sounded like "Bushwhackers!"

The surge of irritation that caused him to reveal his presence now grew into a full burst of anger. How could one little stupid man be so canny? Feeling secure in his exit plan, he decided to try a shot.

As he brought his rifle barrel down and began to align the sights on Peewee's chest, he suffered a repeat of the same experience he had the last time he had tried to shoot Peewee. Flying tree bark burned his cheek and temporarily blinded him in his right eye. He got his shot off and it whined off the iron wagon tire of the right rear wheel. The misshapen bullet buried itself in the side of the wagon bed.

Bing fully exposed himself as he, in his confusion, ran at a right angle to the planned exit route that would have immediately dropped him out of sight. Peewee's rifle cracked a second time, and Bing felt a sharp sting across his back just below his shoulder blades at the same moment that he stumbled on a rock and fell headlong. That stumble saved his life. Otherwise, the piece of hot lead would have pierced his chest from his right side to the left side.

As he fell, his rifle tumbled some ten feet ahead, and he didn't try to retrieve it. Having regained his sense of direction, he crawled down the ridge to his left and then ran to his horse. The men on the wagons, now off the wagons and in position behind trees, heard the hoof beats of a running horse. They did not immediately leave cover, but continued to look and listen.

Finally, Mr. Marlow said, "Let's check it out. We will see if the sign he left tells us anything."

"It was Bully," Peewee said. "He tried to shoot me."

"How do you know it was Bully?" Marlow asked. "We didn't get that good a look at him."

"I could tell by the way he moved," Peewee insisted.

When they saw the abandoned rifle, Peewee recognized it as Bully's rifle. "You skinned this tree," Marlow's partner said. "That may explain why he ran to one side. He was probably partially blinded."

Peewee was looking at some blood at chest level on a bush down the slope. "He left blood on that bush as he squeezed by it," he said. "I cut him across the back. He stumbled just as I pulled the trigger."

On the way back to the wagons, Marlow mulled over what had happened. Neither he nor his partner had seen Bully until after Peewee shot. Peewee had skinned the tree where Bully was taking sight on him. His sharp eyes spotted just a small bit of blood on a bush that told him the second shot burned Bully across the back. If Bully had not stumbled, that second shot would have finished him. Marlow gained an increased respect for Peewee.

When they got to the Marlow barn, Bobby Jack quickly filled them in on developments there. Peewee recognized the footprints as belonging to Bully. All of Bing's murderous efforts became glaringly obvious. "He thought you were sleeping in the harness room," Marlow said. "I wonder how he got that information."

The next day Marlow, Peewee and Bobby Jack were astride the Marlow horses headed toward Peewee's farm. Bing was at the farm, but he was making preparations to leave. He was in the worst of moods and looking for an opportunity to lash out. His horse had become fearful of him, but Bing was blind to the danger that lay in that fear.

Yancey had left while Bing slept. Bing could not understand how he managed to leave without his knowing it. Because of the pain across his back, he had slept very little. Yancey cleaned the wound as best he could and then applied some honey to it. He kept a jar of honey to sweeten his coffee, and it also came in handy in the event of a cut or scrape. It helped prevent infection and hastened healing.

Yancey had come to distrust his younger brother. It was not just one or two things, but a series of incidents that could not be readily explained away. Bing was the only family he knew about, and he wanted to maintain the family tie. That desire had led him to accept vague explanations and questionable circumstances that he would not have accepted from anyone else.

Going back to his arrest that led to eight years in prison, it was Bing's riotous ways that led the arresting officers to him. Somehow, Bing had slipped away and Yancey gave him due credit for accomplishing that. Lately, however, he had begun to wonder if Bing had succeeded in that effort by deliberately using him to deflect attention from himself. Bing was so much like their mother, and that was the sort of thing she would do with no hesitation and no pangs of conscience.

Even though Yancey cracked safes, he had his own moral code. Loyalty was one of the principles he valued, and he didn't want to give up on his brother. After his father died, his father's wealthy friends began to treat him with disdain, if they even acknowledged his presence at all. His resentment gnawed at him, and he longed for a way to get back at them.

He landed a job with a locksmith and after a year had passed, the locksmith began to treat him as if he was family. He suffered strong pangs of conscience at violating the trust the locksmith placed in him, but his resentment toward his father's wealthy friends was stronger. He gained a satisfaction from stealing from them that went beyond the monetary gain.

Bing had contradicted himself twice in describing the business arrangements with Harland, and Yancey had questioned Bing as to why he had not negotiated better prices. He was beginning to wonder if his brother was holding out on him.

He became very suspicious when Bing hinted that Harland might not pay for the next delivery at all.

Although he did not mention it to Bing, he noticed that Bing did not bring his rifle back with him. Bing took great pride in that rifle and his ability to use it. Yancey did not ask him about it because he did not believe Bing would tell him the truth. He did not care to hear a lie.

Bing's explanation for the wound did not satisfy him at all. According to Bing, he rode into the path of a bullet that a half-grown boy fired at a raccoon. Bing having brought law officers down on him once before, Yancey didn't want to take the chance of it happening again. He could only wonder who might be pursuing Bing this time, and what might be the reason for the pursuit. It was time to go.

Even so, he estimated the value of each item in their loot bags from the three last burglaries, and he left Bing half of it. He had clung to the idea of family loyalty well beyond the point at which he felt comfortable in doing so. Now, the time had come to make the break and to make it permanent. It left him with a desolate feeling.

Bing, however, felt only anger that Yancey had put him down. Yancey left nothing in writing, but the message could not have been plainer. Bing never expected to see him again, but only one part of that bothered him. He needed Yancey's skills for a few more months.

His back stung and hurt, his horse was acting up, and his right eye hurt from the bullet-driven bark that struck it the day before. Moreover, he was not at all clear in his own mind as to where to go and what to do. It would be another week before Harland killed Weber, and he didn't have the patience to wait that long. He just might do the job himself and then skip out to distant parts.

With his part of the money from the earlier sale to Harland, plus the money he had withheld from Yancey, he had a pretty good road stake. When he got to distant parts, he could safely sell the items Yancey had left. That Weber kid had become an obsession with him, and he had to get rid of him before he left. Of course, he was no longer a kid, and as much as he hated it, raw fear ran through him at that thought.

Ambush! That was the way he preferred to work. He was an excellent shot with a rifle, although not quite as good as he liked to believe. He couldn't imagine how Peewee had spotted him, and although he had run the scenario through his mind repeatedly, he couldn't come up with an answer. The angry gesture he had made with his right fist at seeing Peewee doing well, remained in his subconscious mind. But Peewee saw it, understood it and remembered it.

But he had no rifle. He had abandoned it in a desperate effort to flee for his life. That was but another fact that fueled his anger. Bing had never learned how to deal with frustration, and he didn't want to learn. He just wanted to lash out at others. Anyone who thwarted him deserved whatever grief he could cause them.

The day was hot, and he had begun to sweat. The sweat stung the wound across his back beneath his shoulder blades, and he cursed his bad luck. He habitually blamed someone else and bad luck when things didn't work out as he planned. He had long since rejected any thoughts that he had any responsibility for any poor results that flowed from his actions.

Although he had carefully planned to cheat and then to abandon his older brother, he faulted his brother for leaving him. While he felt free to treat anyone else in any way he wanted, if any person either deliberately or unwittingly interfered with his plans, he felt completely justified in being angry at that person. He cursed Yancey again and again. When he wasn't cursing Yancey, he cursed his horse.

Peewee spoke just loud enough for Marlow and Bobby Jack to hear. "Wait! Stop!" Then they heard what Peewee had heard. A fast walking horse was coming around the curve ahead and the rider was cursing. Peewee recognized that voice.

"Y'all move on off to the side!" He spoke in an uncharacter-istically authoritative voice. "That's Bully, and it's better to meet him now in broad daylight than when he sneaks up on me at night." Peewee jumped off his horse and tethered him quickly to a nearby sapling. He stepped back into the middle of the road with his rifle at the ready.

When Bing rounded the curve and sighted the small body of Peewee standing in the middle of the road with his feet slight-ly spread and his body turned at an angle ready to shoot, he could not have experienced any greater shock. All his pent-up anger turned to stark fear in one stunning moment. The rifle in Peewee's hands was not yet pointed at him, and there was but one overriding thought in Bing's mind. He had to get out of the road before that rifle barrel was, indeed, trained on him.

The bits tore at the horse's mouth as Bing plow-reined his horse to the right and down into the dry stream bed that ran alongside the road. Unwilling to shoot a fleeing man in the back, Peewee let him go. He was tempted to shoot him just to spare his horse the mistreatment. Peewee seldom got any angrier than when he saw a horse or mule treated badly.

Remembering the sniper attempt the day before and the tracks in the barn lot, Marlow expected Peewee to cut him down. He would not have blamed him at all, even though Bing was fleeing and the shot would have been in the back. Marlow became thoughtful when Peewee held his fire. There was more to this little man than anyone had ever imagined.

SURPRISES, BOTH GOOD AND BAD

I made the trip alone that day from the Scroggins house to mine. Brenda Ann worked with two cousins to dry peach slices in the bright hot sun. I spent the day building strong little crates in which to put jars of honey for shipping. By the time the honey rode by wagon to Springfield, or anywhere else for that matter, it had to take a lot of jostling and shaking. Ozark roads were not known for being smooth.

On my way back, the late afternoon was still, humid and hot. In spite of the heat, Rusty and Cajun wanted to tag along, and I felt inclined, for some reason, to let them. I usually sent them back home after the first mile. Well, "tag along" isn't exactly the right term. Actually they ranged back and forth ahead of me a hundred feet up to a hundred yards.

Of course, everyone knows that a dog doesn't sweat and relies on a dripping tongue for cooling. I didn't want them to get overheated, so I held Dutch to a steady unhurried walk. Probably because of the heat, he seemed contented to amble along slowly. There was no breeze at all, but I had the feeling that things would change before daybreak. It just felt like a storm was likely to follow, and we needed the rain.

Suddenly Dutch's ears pointed forward on full alert, and he stopped walking. I pulled my Winchester from the boot while searching for what he had seen or heard. Rusty was almost to the huge body of the big walnut tree when he smelled Bing. He began to bark and snarl and Cajun came to join him in long lopes. The tree was no more than eight feet from the road, and it was plain that he intended to shoot me point blank before I had a chance to react.

Bing must have been twelve to fifteen years older than I, and I couldn't help but sympathize with him as he ran at his top speed up that slope on such a sultry hot day. I called the dogs off because I didn't want to chance their being shot. I couldn't shoot a running man in the back, even though he obviously intended to kill me in an ambush.

If, however, he had turned to shoot either Rusty or Cajun, I would have done my best to take him out. The intervening trees up the slope would have made him a difficult target. The dogs had done their job by flushing him out, and that action probably saved my life. Dutch alerted me, but that might not have been enough because Bing was completely concealed behind the big tree.

Soon I heard cursing and the neighing of a horse in distress. Then I heard his hoofs pounding the ground as if he were bucking. It wasn't difficult to imagine Bing rushing back to his horse and then jerking the horse around in his frustration. He must have succeeded in getting into the saddle, and now his horse was trying to dislodge him. That a horse was expending that kind of energy in this heat didn't bode well for the horse.

Then came the sound of the horse galloping at full speed, and I felt sorry for the horse. He couldn't last in this heat. Dutch was drenched with sweat even at a slow walk. As the sound of the hoof beats grew fainter, they suddenly ceased. I could hear Bing cursing. With the dogs ranging ahead of us, Dutch carried me slowly up the slope where Bing had tethered his horse. The ground was marred and torn by the hooves of the bucking horse, and the tracks of a galloping horse led around the hill to a less severe slope.

We continued cautiously along the trail, and after almost a half mile we found the horse lying on its side. It was trembling and breathing quick shallow breaths. I poured water from my water bag around its mouth and nose and managed to get a trickle into its throat, but my efforts were futile. The horse was dying. Cajun and Rusty followed Bing's tracks farther on the trail, but I called them back.

Now that the bushwhacker was afoot, he would be desperate for a horse. I had to warn the neighbors. But first I was curious about the contents of the saddlebag pinned underneath the horse. The other saddlebag had been emptied of its contents and left open. Bing had tried to pry the horse upward with a rotten limb, using a rock as a fulcrum.

I succeeded in releasing the girth, and looped my rope around the saddle horn. Dutch made quick work of separating the saddle from the horse. I pulled a canvas sack from the leather, and put it in my own saddle bag. The neck of the canvas bag was tightly wound about with leather string. I would find a better time to examine the contents.

The dogs continued to range ahead of me as we made our way to the Scroggins place. They had very possibly saved my life once today, and they might do it again. Although they did not remove the necessity for my own watchful eye, they would likely spot danger before I did. The sun had gone down, and it would soon be dark.

Upon quickly warning Brenda Ann and her cousins, I headed back to my place. Toby would see to it that the word spread from there. To ring a bell would just put people and horses on the road and make it easier for Bing to seize a horse. Moreover, the bell would clearly notify him that horses would be coming.

It was dark when I got back to my house, and a breeze was beginning to stir the leaves. It was surely building up to storm. A strange horse stood at the hitching post. I soon learned that Lou Evelyn had a caller. One of the young men building the house for Toby and Peggy Frances had come to see her, and they were sitting in rocking chairs on the front porch.

Barnabas, who everyone called "Barney," immediately volunteered to spread the word through the community. "I have my slicker on my horse. We will probably get a good rain by midnight, unless I miss my guess." He paused thoughtfully. "He may be looking to wait out the storm in somebody's barn. If he can get the drop on them, he might barge into somebody's house to get some food."

"He left his slicker on his horse," I volunteered. "He might find a cave to get out of the weather, but he won't find a horse or food in a cave."

"I will set a watch in the barn," Toby said. "The women can take turns staying awake in the house. We would all like to get some sleep, but this scumbag may try anything. I don't know of anyone who can afford to lose a horse and saddle."

I reined Dutch around to leave and said my farewells. "Keep the dogs with you," Toby added. "They may save your bacon again."

Before I reached the public road the dogs barked and growled at something that lay beside the public road on the other side. It was Harland. We weren't expecting him for another week. He had been knocked from his horse with a section of an old oak limb that had been left from the cutting of firewood.

Knocked unconscious, he was coming to his senses. He remembered only that in the darkness a man had asked him for help, saying that his horse had thrown him. The voice sounded familiar, but he could not place it. I left him there to return to the house for help. Except for my bad leg, I would have simply helped him to the house.

Barney had already left in the opposite direction, so Toby quickly saddled his horse. Although he was still dizzy and somewhat disoriented, Harland was able to stay in the saddle.

He had no broken bones, but his right shoulder hurt from his fall on the rocky ground.

Only then did the question cross my mind: Why was he at the southwest end of my private road? Access to the community was gained from the northwest, and he bypassed the northwest entrance. Or was he coming from the direction of the Scroggins place? If so, why?

Again at the house, while Betty Jean was washing the back of his head where the limb had struck him, he repeated the statement he had made to me. "The voice sounded familiar. Otherwise, I might have been more cautious. I still can't recall where I heard it before, but it has to be one of your neighbors."

Betty Jean stiffened, and her jaw set hard. For a moment I wondered if she was going to give him another blow to the back of his head. The moment passed, and in an indulgent tone she said, "We trust all our neighbors around here, but one never knows. Sometimes a person you trust will turn out to be someone you never imagined."

Peggy Frances started to tell Harland about my experience, but Betty Jean silenced her by shaking her head and placing her right index finger over her lips. Peggy Frances smoothly led off into another subject, and Harland seemed to have no curiosity about my "close call."

So Bing now had a horse and saddle. What would he do now? Would he leave the country, or would he hang around for more devilment? He probably knew now that I had taken possession of the canvas sack. What was in the sack? Was it worth coming back for?

I suddenly realized I was tired, and my bad leg was aching. "I will see you folks tomorrow," I said. "I may be a little later than usual."

Before I could get out the door Harland became very interested in my plans for the next day, and he wanted to know where he could buy a good horse and saddle. Money didn't seem to pose a problem for him. He also declared his intention to buy a couple of changes of clothes and a rifle. "The thief took my new rifle," he said.

He asked me to go with him to make his purchases. Toby interceded. "Rick's leg still bothers him a lot, and he's had a full day today. He needs to rest it tomorrow. I will saddle a horse for you and go with you."

A flash of irritation crossed Harland's face. "I would just like to get better acquainted with my future brother-in-law." he said. "I have developed a lot of respect for him."

It was Betty Jean's turn to show irritation. "You are announcing our engagement, and I have not consented to marry you." Her voice had a confident and matter-of-fact quality that I had not heard before, and by Harland's reaction, the tone was apparently new to him. He seemed to actually shrink a little bit.

He made an effort to regain his poise. "Oh, when you see the wedding ring I have bought for you, it won't take you long to say 'yes.' The thief didn't get that. It's in my pocket. I got a real good buy on it."

Betty Jean's voice was cold. "When I marry, it won't be for a ring. And right now, I have no idea who I will marry."

Before he had an opportunity to respond, she stepped quickly into the bedroom she shared with Lou Evelyn, and she shut the door behind her. Harland seemed stunned, but he tried to brush it off. "I forgot," he said. "Women like romance, formal proposals and such. That blow on the head must have addled my brain. I will talk to her tomorrow after she's had a chance to get over my clumsy approach."

As if he had not heard what Toby said about giving my leg a rest, he began again to try to persuade me to ride along with him to replace what he had lost to Bing. What would he think if he remembered where he had heard that voice?

His insistence on having me ride along with him puzzled me. Living alone for seven years had made me keen to anything that departed from the usual ebb and flow, anything that was different from the customary give and take. I was suddenly wary.

"You just got here," I told him, "and you are probably going to be sore from that fall. Just wait a day or two, and I will go with you. There is no reason to be in a rush. Take time to visit."

Sukey was seated behind and to the left of Harland. She pointed at Harland with her right hand and mouthed the words, "You watch him. Be careful." I had learned to trust Sukey's judgment in people. She had learned her lessons from hard experience. I believe she was having an influence on Betty Jean.

Clayton Hardeway came to see Sukey regularly now, and they had long talks under the stars. It seemed that the only obstacle to their relationship leading to marriage was Clayton's nine-year-old daughter. She took a hard stance against her father remarrying. Sukey told Clayton that she would not move into his house over his daughter's objections.

Clayton had a seven-year-old son who liked Sukey, and he argued with his sister about her attitude. He called her "bossy" and scolded her about being selfish and stubborn. The daughter had carefully assembled her mother's personal items in her own bedroom, and she spent time brooding over them. "She's still grieving," Sukey told Clayton. "We have to find a way to help the child through that grief so that she will look forward to living her life. My moving in might cause her to spiral in the other direction."

When I called Rusty and Cajun from under the front porch, they were reluctant to come out. They knew where I was headed, and they had already covered quite a few miles this day. More than that, I suspect they did not want to get drenched. Thunder was rumbling in the distance.

I did not like riding in a thunderstorm. Any sensible person fears the lightning. Large tall trees lined the road to the Scroggins place, and there was a measure of protection in that fact. A horseman in an open pasture or field is a prime target for a lightning strike. But there was also danger in riding near trees. A nearby tree might be the one to attract a lightning strike.

I considered letting them stay at home, but I had come to rely on their ability to smell, see and hear. Bing was probably settled in for the night in someone's barn, and it might be the Scroggins barn. He might know of a cave, but it was certain that he would be seeking some kind of shelter from the storm. If Bing was in the Scroggins barn, he would have more than shelter in mind. He would anticipate my arrival there.

We had covered about half of the distance when the first drops of rain fell, and I could hear the rain moving toward us. I put on my slicker just in time. A torrent of water began to fall. Between the flashes of lightning, the night was pitch black. I couldn't see the dogs, but I had confidence that they were ranging ahead of Dutch and me. Dutch knew where we were headed, and I let him choose the exact path and speed.

When Dutch and I were about seventy-five yards from the barn, Rusty and Cajun began to snarl and bark, and I recognized Bing's voice cursing his "luck." I heard the back gate of the barn slam shut. That would put Bing and Harland's horse on the opposite side of the gate from the dogs, and it also put him in the cow pasture. I heard the horse slopping through mud puddles in the darkness.

I made a mental note to check the fence the next morning. Bing would leave a section of rails taken down so that he and his stolen horse could pass through. I also made a mental note to check the canvas bag I had taken from his dead horse. I left it earlier with Brenda Ann. Its contents might be the reason for his presence.

I unsaddled Dutch and wiped him off with hay. My leg ached and weariness tempted me to do a halfway job of rubbing him down, but I knew he was tired too. My conscience wouldn't let me leave him half wet. When a man takes good care of his animals, they will usually repay him for his efforts.

Brenda Ann was waiting up for me with a relieved look on her face. It did something for me deep inside to know that I had someone who was concerned about me. I had permitted this relationship to develop between us when I knew that I might not be able to follow through. Now I knew that I had to finish the job I had started or die trying. For one thing, she had demonstrated that she was more than equal to the rigorous demands of living close to the land in The Ozarks. But not only that. She loved it.

I found some leftovers from supper and got her consent to give them to Rusty and Cajun. Except for them, Bing might have successfully ambushed and killed me in the barn. He could have found shelter elsewhere, but his choice of the Scroggins barn must have had a reason, perhaps more than one reason. I had to check the canvas bag first thing in the morning.

I slept soundly, trusting to the dogs to alert us to any intruders. Brenda Ann possessed keen hearing, and she slept lightly, so I felt secure in going into a deep sleep. I needed the rest. Fortunately, after a few minutes in the bed, my injured leg quit aching. In spite of my intention to sleep an hour late, I awakened at the usual time, feeling refreshed and hungry.

The canvas bag was secured at the top by three different leather strings that had been wound and tied tightly, so tightly that I chose to cut them. I wanted to open the bag in the presence of witnesses because I felt sure it contained stolen items. Brenda Ann and her two female cousins collectively caught their breaths when I poured the contents onto the table.

I knew nothing of jewelry and had never had any interest in learning. In the Ozark hills, we were more practical, even the more prosperous women. Married women typically wore only a plain gold wedding band, if they wore one at all. Daily work requirements dictated that a ring with diamonds was worn only on special occasions. There were daily cleaning, washing, gardening, cooking and numerous other tasks that made the wearing of jewelry impractical.

Brenda Ann and her cousins, however, had moved among affluent women who did little physical work and had the financial means to acquire expensive pieces of jewelry. They were free to wear the jewelry on a regular basis, although neither Brenda Ann nor her cousins seemed inclined in that direction. In fact, they emulated Mrs. Scroggins who loved gardening and the usual physical tasks of maintaining a country household.

Out on the table rolled a collection of jewelry that even I could see was worth a small fortune. Bing had moved from horse stealing to something much more lucrative. I was to learn later that it represented only about half of what was taken in three separate burglaries. When we put the jewelry in the hands of the sheriff, he immediately connected it to a series of burglaries that had occurred across a wide area.

As time went by, they determined that this particular bag contained items from only three of those burglaries, and only about half of that. That immediately brought me under suspicion of holding back part of the loot, although they readily accepted my account of how I came into possession of it. The canvas bag would easily have held more than twice the contents we found in it, and that was a factor in the suspicion the rightful owners directed toward us.

One of the couples who had suffered the loss readily believed our account and showed their gratitude with a generous cash reward. My parents had drilled into me the attitude that I should neither want nor accept what I had not earned. I declined their offer, but they insisted that I had, in fact, earned the reward. Brenda Ann stepped forward and explained to them that I was orphaned at the age of twelve and had supported myself for the ensuing "growing-up" years. "You have never seen anyone as independent-minded as he is," she declared.

She then explained to me in their presence that declining their offer was less than gracious. Well, what could I do? Words from Brenda Ann's mouth carried special weight. She suggested to me, again in their presence, that I use the money to construct a well-equipped honey house. They were fascinated when they learned that I was a beekeeper and honey producer. It turned out that they had purchased some of my honey.

Privately, she suggested to me that the suspicions of the other two couples were not real, but an excuse for not offering a reward for the recovery. "When money is involved," she said, "you learn who people really are. When money is at stake, it strips away the false facades and reveals character."

Later she said something that I can hear ringing in my ears to this day. "When I first met you, Rick, I knew that principle would always be first with you, that there wasn't enough money in the world to make you violate your basic principles. I was concerned that one of those principles, your independence, might prevent me from being a part of your life. That's what worried me most about you."

But that was several months later. Right now, according to Brenda Ann and her two cousins, we were looking at a small fortune in stolen jewelry. I wanted it off my hands, and the sooner the better. Again, trusting Cajun and Rusty to alert me to danger, I rode to my place. It was one of those fresh cool days that often follows a summer storm, a good day to be alive. I thanked my Lord above that I was, indeed, alive.

Mr. Marlow and Bobby Jack were there, and I learned about the assassination attempt on Peewee. That Bing would make a second attempt on Peewee after failing at his nighttime effort at the Marlow barn, showed that he had determination. They explained that Bing had a partner, but somehow Peewee had deduced that the partner had abandoned him in the middle of the night. He also declared that the partner was someone not known to him.

It surprised me to learn that Peewee owned a small farm inherited from his grandmother. In a single action-filled day both he and Sukey had become major parts of our lives. I had no doubt that they had both put their outlaw days behind them. They both seemed enthused about their new lifestyles.

I showed the jewelry to Toby and Mr. Marlow, and they both admonished me that I had no business carrying that small fortune alone. "He might guess that you are headed to the Sheriff, and he may recruit help to stop you," Mr. Marlow said.

Toby suggested that he and Marlow ride along with me, but Mr. Marlow suggested that Peewee go along in his place. "There just ain't much that little guy misses," he said. "And he can shoot."

Our conversation took place in the front yard near the hitching post, just the three of us. Bobby Jack had gone inside to see Peggy Frances and Sukey. Harland came to the front door as I was retying the leather cord around the neck of the canvas bag. When he saw the bag, he froze and his face lost its natural color. He quickly backed into the house and closed the door. The three of us looked at one another with puzzled expressions.

When we reached the Marlow homestead, Peewee was in the middle of working with the mules, checking their feet and shoes and clipping their manes. He seemed reluctant to interrupt his work until he learned about the perceived threat from Bing, "Bully" to him. Before mounting his horse, he checked his rifle and six-shooter carefully.

Peewee seemed thoughtful as we rode, but his eyes constantly scanned the landscape ahead. Occasionally he turned to look behind us. We had told him what we were delivering and how it came into my possession. Finally, he broke his silence.

"When Bully would get out of sorts with us about something, which happened real regular, he would tell us he was going to ditch us one day. He said he had a brother in the big house who could bust any safe they made, and he knew where there were some safes just waiting to be busted. That must have been who was camping with him on my place. But it looks like Bully was the one who got ditched."

Peewee seldom said more than one or two sentences at a time. This was like a major discourse for him, and we had learned to listen when he spoke. He didn't talk just to hear himself talk or to pass the time of day. "How did you figure the partner left him?" I asked.

"His tracks and those of his horses --- he had a packhorse --- were several hours older than Bully's," he answered. "I have seen Bully stomp around when he was mad about something. He would tear up the ground pretty good. He did that when he discovered his partner was gone."

We rode for a while without speaking, just remaining alert to the country around us. We met an occasional wagon and several lone horsemen, and we would swap a "Howdy!" with them in passing. I noticed that Peewee treated them warily and kept his distance from them while, at the same time, checking every nook and cranny both in front and behind.

Finally Peewee spoke again. "It's a pretty sure bet that Bully is going try again to get that jewelry," he said. He pointed northeast with his free right hand. "Out that way about two miles there's an old man that Bully would get to help us sometimes. He lives in a little cabin by himself, and he would keep some horses for us when we needed that. He may get him to help hit us. We better be watching everybody real close."

"How do you think the two of them would work together to hit us?" Toby asked.

A crow called and Peewee held up his hand for silence. The crow called a second time, and then a third call was followed by silence. "That's Bully," Peewee declared. "I've heard that call before."

Then he replied to Toby's question. "Might not be just the two of them. The old man probably knows somebody else who would help for a few dollars. When we meet somebody on the road, it may be somebody working with Bully. I would recognize the old man, but it might not be him."

We all rode along quietly, watchful and silent. After a short distance, we heard the rumblings of a wagon, its wheels clicking and clucking over the rocky roadway. I immediately became suspicious because when we first heard the wagon it was near us, just around the curve ahead. It had been stopped for some reason.

When the wagon came into view, Peewee said urgently, "This is it! That's not the old man, but those are his mules and his wagon. And there's a slow-walking horse behind us."

Marlow was absolutely right about Peewee not missing much. I had not heard the slow-walking horse. There was a curve ahead of us and a curve behind us. It was a likely place to pull this kind of maneuver. After Peewee called my attention to the slow-walking horse, I heard it. Then I heard it stop just short of the point at which the horse and rider would be visible to us.

"You fellows take care of what is up ahead," Peewee said in a voice full of confidence and authority. "I will handle the rear."

Toby and I continued riding two abreast, while Peewee lagged behind. I put a little more space between Toby and me, and he did the same. "Howdy," called the wagon driver as he stopped the wagon and began to wind the reins around a peg to his left. "You fellas have any tobaccy? I've run plumb out, and I need a smoke bad." His right hand hung out of sight behind the front end-gate. I could now see a canvas sheet in the wagon bed with something under it.

"Better get the drop on them now," I told Toby. We were within six-shooter range, so I brought my pistol to bear on the driver. I heard Peewee's horse spin and begin a running walk in the opposite direction. I saw movement under the tarp. He was getting ready to throw it off at any moment.

"You guys know that fellow behind us?" I asked them.

"There's just me, nobody else," he lied. "And I need a smoke. There's no call to go pointing your pistols at me." He was a well-dressed middle-aged paunchy fellow. Most Ozarkers were slender from so much walking up and down the hills. He had the looks of a newcomer.

I turned Dutch at a right angle to the driver, enabling me to check on Peewee. Toby hung back and turned his horse at a better angle to watch both directions. We saw Bing come into view with a rifle in hand and ready. That must be the rifle he took from Harland. When he saw Peewee, who already had his rifle trained on him, he released the rifle as if it might have been red hot.

He spun his horse and headed back in the opposite direction at an all-out gallop. There had been numerous opportunities to take Bing out, but no one was willing to shoot him in the back. Peewee turned to check on us, and then he retrieved the rifle Bing had discarded so hastily.

Toby urged his horse to near the center of the wagon on his side. "Now I would really hate to shoot up a nice-looking canvas sheet and the floor of the wagon, but if you don't come out from under that wagon sheet, that's exactly what I'm going to do," Toby declared.

I told the driver, "If you want to live, you will slowly move your hand away from that shotgun. Slow and easy." His eyes were big, and he seemed more than happy to comply. This had not worked out the way they had planned.

A skinny old man slowly moved the canvas away and reached for the sideboard to pull himself to a sitting position. "How

123

much did Bully pay you for this?" Toby inquired. "Or have you collected yet?"

The old man looked dejected, but he was defensive. "I was jes tryin' to help a friend git somethin' back that rightfully belongs to him. I jes' hate that we failed."

"So that's his line," I thought. "He probably has long experience at putting a good face on evil actions."

Peewee looked down from his horse. "Slingshot," he said, "you know Bully don't have a thing he didn't steal. He just talked you into helping him rob somebody, and you didn't care for anything but what he paid you. I hope you got paid in advance."

"Peewee, that's you!" Slingshot exclaimed. "Bully said you might be along, but I didn't recognize you. Now, Peewee, a lot of people treated you bad, but you know old Slingshot always treated you right."

"So you signed on to help him kill me? Is that treating me right?"

I could tell that Peewee's accusation hit home. The glib old man was at a loss for words for a moment, but not for long. "Now is that any way to talk to an old friend?" He whined.

"We are going to take your guns with us," I said. "We ought to take the two of you along to spend time in the hoosegow, but we just don't want to mess with you. We are going to make a full report to the sheriff, though."

I pointed the barrel of my pistol at first one and then the other. They cringed, wondering just what I had in mind. "We will come back from town on this same road. If we see you, we will take no chances. We all three hit what we shoot at. Don't make us have to shoot at you."

I paused a moment to let it sink in. "If you want to live, you will remain very still while Toby collects your guns and frisks you for any hideouts. If this thing had played out the way you planned, we three would be dead now. We won't forget that."

"And there's something the two of you might turn over in your crooked minds. You would probably be dead too. This was a perfect setup for Bully to take out the two of you as soon as you got us. He's tried to kill Peewee three times simply because he knows too much. The same thing applies to you. You might think about that when he comes around later today, mad at you for failing to take us out."

The blood seemed to drain from the paunchy man's face. In a plaintive voice he said, "You are taking our guns. We have no way to defend ourselves."

"Find a hole that Bully doesn't know about until he leaves the country," I said "His safe-cracking partner put him down, so he will probably move on to new territory."

"Safe-cracking!" Slingshot's chin jerked upward from his bony chest. "Stealing a few horses here and there, now that's one thing. But cracking safes? These rich people won't put up with that! They won't leave that to the sheriff. They will hire a whole bevy of private dicks."

The whining paunchy guy spoke up. "He was already mad when he showed up this morning. He was almighty sore about something. If we had not agreed to help him, I believe he would have shot us on the spot. He didn't ask us; he told us."

A thought was running through my mind. I didn't want it on my conscience that they were slaughtered with no means to defend themselves. "Slingshot, I'm sure you have more guns and ammunition at home and probably at two or three other spots, but I don't want you to get your liver blown to smithereens on your way home. Bully dropped his rifle to keep Peewee from shooting him out of the saddle, so he probably has only his six-shooter left."

I had their full attention now. They were hanging on my every word. "We will put your pistols and the shotgun on that big stump up ahead. After you get your wagon turned around, you can pick them up. Just remember what I said. If we see you on our return trip, we will take it that you are not friendly, and we will act accordingly."

Slingshot looked me straight in the eye. "Weber, Ole Slingshot won't forget this. You've got reason to leave us laying here in the road with open eyes that don't see anything. We won't forget that you gave us a break."

"Got to be going," I said. "You better keep a sharp lookout. Bully may be circling back right now."

The sheriff acted downright jubilant over our delivery to him. "This is the first break in a case that has moneyed people threatening sheriffs in four different counties. They get very unhappy when their safes get busted."

Peewee decided to contribute his knowledge. "Bully talked about having a brother in the big house who would get out soon. He said he would ditch all of us when that happened. He had a partner, probably that brother, who ditched him. We found their camp the day he woke up to find his partner gone. He stomped all around and tore up the ground."

"Now that is a real break!" the sheriff replied. "We can check to see if a safe cracker has been released in the last several months."

"We all knew Bully as Bing Hodges," I said. "He worked for the Robinsons."

The sheriff jumped out of his chair. "What!!! The one you took a buggy whip from when you were only fourteen? After the Robinsons fired him, he just dropped out of sight. I figured he had gone to some other state hundreds of miles from here."

"That new colt pistol that I sent to your office was dropped by Bing at my place when he was trying to shoot me. You didn't get that message?"

"I was out of town when that pistol came in. I never did understand who sent it or why. Insofar as I'm concerned you can have it back, but I guess I had better hold on to it for a while. It might have some connection to this case."

The sheriff paused, obviously thinking. Then his eyes lit up. "The Robinsons probably know every one of the people whose safes have been robbed. Bing went everywhere with them, driving that surrey. Things are adding up."

Toby had been standing at the door where he could watch our horses. He decided to speak up. "Sheriff, Bing tried to get that jewelry back as we were bringing it in this morning. Rick was going to bring it in alone, but Peewee and I decided to ride along to help out if needed. We guessed right, and we have a new rifle outside that he dropped when he saw that Peewee had him in his sights."

"He's right here in the county now? I will get some men together, and we will try to catch him. Bring that rifle in, and I will try to find out where it was bought. If he has lost his rifle, this would be a good time to apprehend him." The sheriff walked to the door and called to someone across the street.

Soon the bank president appeared. "Jim," the sheriff told him, "this bag contains a small fortune in stolen jewelry. I need you to keep it for me in your bank safe. Make a list of what it contains and get that to me. I appreciate your help."

A deputy strode in behind the banker, and the sheriff named three men he wanted to join with them in the search for Bing. "They won't be long getting here," he said. "The five of us want to ride along with you on the way back so you can show us exactly where you last saw him."

I made no comment on what I thought their chances were of catching Bing. Now, if he deputized Peewee and let him go after him alone, Peewee would probably bring him back either dead or alive. The group of five would favorably impress the voters, and that just might be the foremost thing on the sheriff's mind. He and other sheriffs were catching criticism from some politically powerful people because they had not solved the string of safecracking burglaries.

I could see no way that five horsemen were going to get close enough to Bing to capture him, but I did see a positive side to the effort. It would convey the message to Bing that he was hot, and maybe he would stay out of the country for a while. And maybe someone would catch him or kill him before he found his way back.

I never wished for any man's death, but Bing had become a real headache. So long as he lived, I would never know when or where he might pop up. I did know that he was not likely to ever be friendly toward me. He was the one who started the altercation when I was fourteen, but he became bitter toward me for the way it ended.

When we reached the place where Bing had dropped the rifle and spurred his horse away from Peewee, the tracks were still plain because his horse's hooves had dug hard into the rocky roadway. Farther along, Peewee spotted tracks with enough detail in them to enable them to identify the horse's tracks when they saw them again. We left them then.

A few miles down the road, Toby made a comment that expressed my own thoughts. "I don't expect the sheriff's efforts to amount to much, but maybe it will help Bing decide to get out of the country."

Peewee immediately responded. "He's a vengeful man. He's mad at me because I'm not still with him doing his bidding and all his dirty work. He's mad at 'that Weber kid' for putting that scar on his face. He may leave for a while, but he will be back if somebody don't kill him." I thought so too.

When I got back to the Scroggins place, it was dusk. Brenda Ann met me at the barn with a shotgun in her hand and a worried look on her face. "Nothing is wrong," she assured me, "but with all that's been going on, I'm just being cautious. I'm relieved to see you back safe and sound." She asked me no questions, and that was like her. She would wait for me to catch her up on the events of my day.

Dutch had to be tired, but he didn't show it. We got him brushed down, fed and watered, and we walked together to the house. I was using only one crutch now, and in many ways that was awkward, but my left hand remained free to carry something and do other things. Soon I would graduate to a walking cane and use it to take some of the weight off my right leg.

"You are tired and hungry," she said matter-of-factly. "I have kept your supper warm. We will put your plate on this tray, and you can sit in the glider with your feet propped up. The water is fresh from the well."

It felt really good to be fussed over that way, especially by Brenda Ann. An uninformed observer would have to conclude that a tired man had come home to his loving wife. As attentive as she was, she maintained a reserve that I couldn't figure. Again, I remembered her words, "Don't take anything for granted."

Her cousins, dressed for bed, came from their bedroom. They were interested in hearing the account of the trip. That saved me from telling the story twice, but I would really rather have shared it in private with Brenda Ann first.

I began by telling them that Bing tried to get the jewels back, and they were all ears as to how we managed to get through with no casualties. "Will you never be free from Bing's hatred?" Brenda Ann's question was not really a question, but an expression of frustration. I knew that it also reflected her affection for me. Affection? Was it perhaps more than just affection?

FLEETING PEACE AND QUIET

The next morning I learned that Harland had left. He bought a horse and an old saddle from Mr. Marlow. Marlow didn't have a horse for sale, but Harland kept upping the bid until he couldn't refuse the offer. I learned from Lou Evelyn that Harland tried to put a guilt trip on Betty Jean at breakfast the previous morning for not being "sweet" to him.

When that didn't work, he called her away from washing the breakfast dishes to go outside for a "talk." He attempted to scold Betty Jean, and that didn't go well at all. He stormed out, walking to the Marlow place. As he left, he taunted Betty Jean with a yellow gold wedding band with a huge diamond set in it. "Take a good look at what you have just lost," he jeered. "There are plenty pretty women out there who will jump at the chance to wear it."

Betty Jean's demeanor was not that of a young woman who had broken up with her suitor. She was relaxed in a way that I had not seen her since she arrived. It was as if she had dropped a heavy load from her shoulders. She and Sukey headed to the barn to shell some corn. They would go together to the grist mill tomorrow and come back with two big sacks of corn meal. With five people in the house and others dropping in to eat, it took constant effort to keep food supplies in the pantry.

There had not been enough water flowing in the creek to keep the grist mill turning before the recent rain. That rain refilled the mill pond and a constant stream was flowing over the rock dam. That was not likely to last long at this time of year, and people would be crowding around the mill waiting their turn. After this grinding, it might be late October or even November before there was enough water to resume grinding.

The rain would spur the beans to bloom again, and we would have some fresh beans in September if we could get a few showers to follow. To me, a pot of fresh lima beans was a pretty sight. During my years alone, I called them "old reliable." By keeping the dry beans picked as soon as they became dry, we encouraged the plants to continue to bloom and bear. The dry beans, seasoned with meat from a pork shoulder, made good eating during the winter months.

Sukey said she was eating better than she had ever eaten in her life. She showed her appreciation by working harder than anyone else. She still wore the shoulder harness the doctor had made for her, but she had discarded the arm sling. Except for heavy lifting, she had full use of her right arm.

She sometimes joked with me about shooting her. I hated the fact that I had shot her, but she declared on several occasions that she was "so grateful" that I didn't let her pull the trigger on Brenda Ann. That had been the only way to stop her. There was just no other option. It had been a close call.

Clayton Hardeway had quit calling on Sukey because of the opposition of his nine-year old daughter. "It looks like I'm gonna just have to wait 'til she gits growed up and finds herself a man," he told Sukey. "That will be seven or eight years. In your situation you can't wait that long."

Learning that I had three fish traps that had been setting high and dry until the recent rains, Sukey volunteered to check them. It was a thing she was familiar with, having often made a trap or two when the gang was camped in one place for a while. "Now that you mention fish," she said, "I'm fish hungry. Got to go to mill tomorrow. I will check them right after breakfast the next morning."

Bobby Jack learned of her plans while she and Betty Jean were gone to mill, and he insisted upon going along with her. He told Peggy Frances, "I will come over here in time for breakfast. Cook enough for me."

"You are not going to like it when Toby and I move to our new house," Peggy Frances teased. "It won't be so easy for you to come and eat my cooking."

"Pa's looking to buy that young gelding out of the Hardeway mare," he responded "He's a real pretty horse, not as pretty as Dutch, but better than 'most any other horse around these parts. He can handle that extra distance in no time at all."

"But he ain't broke," Peggy Frances countered.

"Looks like I got to catch you up on things, Sis. We got Pee-wee now. He will have that gelding trained and smoothed out in just two or three weeks."

Peggy Frances was serious. "He's that good, really? I heard that he was good."

I put in my penny's worth. "Yeah, Peggy Frances. He's that good. I believe this is the first time in Peewee's life that any-one has ever taken him seriously. And he's showing his stuff."

I was thinking about how Pa had taught me all kinds of little things as we did things around the farm. I couldn't imagine a boy growing up without a responsible man in his life. As I tacked together another small crate for the honey, I expressed my thoughts.

"All the little things that Pa showed me and taught me from the time I can first remember just may be the largest part of who I am today. A boy who grows up without a good man in his life starts life severely handicapped. Peewee didn't have that. Somehow, he found strength and purpose in working with horses and mules."

"But he did have a good man in his life," Bobby Jack interjected. I felt my head pop up and my hands just quit moving all on their own.

"What? Who?" I blurted out.

"Give me time and I'll tell you," he said. I knew he didn't mean it disrespectfully. My surprise had caused me to be abrupt, and I apologized to him.

"He put meat on the table for him and his grandma by hunting with an old rifle and by fishing. He ran into an old man down the creek who trained horses and mules for people. In between times he hunted and fished like Peewee did. He took a liking to Peewee and taught him what he knew about horses and mules."

"Was he married?" Peggy Frances asked.

"When Peewee got to know him, his wife had been dead for several years. He couldn't stand to keep on living in the house they had shared with one another, so he built him a little cabin down on the creek. He taught Peewee a lot of things about hunting and fishing and reading sign."

"What happened to him? How long did Peewee know him?" Peggy Frances inquired.

"He was running around the corral with a horse when he just fell over and died on the spot. Peewee was with him, and he rode a horse three miles to tell the nearest neighbor. He found out then that he was eighty-seven years old. They called him "Quicksilver."

Again I was startled. Quicksilver was a legend, and I had heard that he lived somewhere in the Ozarks. Born in 1790, he rode with General John Coffee at New Orleans in December of 1814 and January of 1815. As late as the Civil War, he worked as a civilian employee of the Quartermaster Corps in charge of procuring top quality horses for the cavalry.

Legend had it that his nickname had been earned by repeatedly surviving dangerous encounters and tough situations. Peewee's friendship with him might well explain how he had become so savvy. I wondered how long their association with one another had lasted, and I asked Bobby Jack.

"They met when Quicksilver shot a squirrel out of a tree just as Peewee was about to pull his trigger on the same squirrel. He didn't know Quicksilver was there, but Quicksilver knew Peewee was about to shoot the squirrel. He laughed at Peewee about it and then gave him the squirrel."

"He told Peewee later that he wouldn't have shot the squirrel if he had known Peewee was such a good shot. He just didn't want the squirrel to get away. Peewee was eight years old then, and they were company to one another for the next five years. Peewee was thirteen when Quicksilver fell dead. I guess I'm the only person Peewee has ever talked to about him."

That much I could readily understand. Peewee had never talked much to anyone until he met Bobby Jack. Bobby Jack went on to explain how Peewee got tied in with Bully.

"Pa talks about how Peewee knows everything that is going on around him all the time. Quicksilver taught him that, and Peewee remembers one time when he got careless. He seldom ever went to town, but when he was twenty-one, two bigger men decided to pick on him because he was little. He gave them both a good thrashing."

"Several months later he was back in town, and they were laying for him. They hit him from behind with a stick of firewood. They pulled him up from the ground while he was still addled, and they began to hit him with their fists. They took turns hitting him and pushing him from one to the other. Bully stepped in and knocked both of them around. He offered Peewee a job when he learned that Peewee worked with horses." Bobby Jack loved to talk, and Peewee had become his favorite subject.

He had even learned Peewee's legal name, "Peter Cornelius Elliott." He said, "I'm thinking I may start calling him 'Pete.' I like that better than 'Peewee.' He may be little, but he's a grown-up man. He deserves some respect."

Peggy Frances agreed, and I thought it was a good idea myself. He had embarked on a new life, and a new moniker would be fitting. "Make it alright with him, and you can count me in," I said. "A proper name is an important thing."

Betty Jean and Sukey got back from the grist mill early because the miller had quite a bit of meal already ground. They just paid the grinding fee and took two of those sacks. "I want to check those fish traps," Sukey said. "Tell me exactly where they are."

Bobby Jack was present when Sukey and Betty Jean got back from the mill. "I know where they are," he offered. "I will go with you. You may need some help." I learned later that she and Bobby Jack spent much of that time together discussing Peewee. She had never learned his real name, and she also liked the idea of calling him "Pete."

They soon returned with an impressive catch of fish, and we all looked forward to eating them. There would be enough for me to take some to Brenda Ann and her cousins. They also brought disturbing news. Harland was still hanging around.

Bobby Jack knew the tracks of the horse Marlow sold to Harland, and he found several clear prints near the creek bank that were made earlier in the day. He and Sukey backtracked the horse and found where he had camped the previous night. They found the butt print of a rifle that had been leaned against a tree in damp soft ground. Harland had acquired a rifle.

I thought of how he had insisted on having me go with him to purchase a horse and outfit, ignoring Toby's suggestion otherwise. Sukey's intuition concerning him confirmed my own suspicions, although I wondered if my personal distaste

136

for him was influencing my judgment. Still, what was he doing hanging around? And it had not taken him long to replace the rifle he had lost to Bing. What was his connection to Bing?

Everybody pitched in to get the fish cleaned and prepared for frying. With five of us working together, all of us with varying degrees of experience, we made quick work of it. I was pleased with how Betty Jean and Lou Evelyn took to Ozark living. Lou Evelyn went into the root cellar and brought back some onions.

Bobby Jack washed out the cast iron wash pot and put four gallons of lard in it. We would strain the lard and save it after cooking the fish. Soon Bobby Jack had a nice fire on the side of the pot from which a steady breeze was blowing. Sukey rolled the fish in salted cornmeal. I soon heard the sound of steam coming from the hot grease when the fish were dropped in. Peggy Frances and Betty Jean had sliced potatoes waiting to follow.

I had to be frugal with the lard until cold weather and hog-killing time. The extra demands for it arising from the extra mouths to feed put us in danger of running out. The hogs I killed were not fat. I preferred them lean, but it took fat hogs to produce much lard.

Like everyone else, my hogs ran loose in the bottoms, and they had to be penned up for a while to make them fat. I eliminated that step because I felt I could find better uses for the corn that made them fat. In any event, the time was upon us that the spring gilts had to be penned to prevent them from breeding too early.

There were people who didn't care for my hams and pork loin because they were too lean to suit their tastes. I didn't eat as much bacon as most people, preferring ham and pork chops for breakfast. I made lard from what would otherwise have become bacon.

My being laid up had prevented me from marking the ears of the pigs when they were small, but I felt I would be able to identify them this fall. There was a problem, though with the male pigs. Nobody wanted to wrestle with a six-month-old male hog to castrate him. On the other hand, nobody wanted to eat the meat from an uncastrated male.

During and after the war almost all the hogs had been killed by people desperate for enough food to survive. The deer and turkey populations had also been greatly diminished. By the time I was born in 1872, those wild game populations had begun to recover. Pa thought it important that I know that history, along with a whole lot more.

He drilled into me the various details of the war between The Union and The Confederacy and the reasons that lay behind it. "You need to know these things," he said, "because history has a tendency to repeat itself." He explained to me that our part of The Ozarks had not been affected as severely as the counties that lay farther south along the Arkansas border. In our part of Missouri, almost everyone supported The Union.

My parents read The Bible with us children, and they taught us to appreciate peace and goodwill among decent, hard-working people. At the same time they stressed the need to be prepared to fight when it became necessary to protect one's families and friends. "Family and friends are worth fighting for," Pa said. "A man who won't do that is not really a man."

This was the kind of industrious peace and quiet I longed for. Everyone seemed to be happy and satisfied with what they were doing, but most of all just contented to be with one another. Ma and Pa would be pleased. They were never far from my mind. I didn't grieve for them anymore; the memory of them was a source of strength.

A customer rolled up in his wagon to pick up some plow-shares that Toby had sharpened and reset for him. The busy season for blacksmith work was winding down, giving Toby a little more time to work at finishing the new home. Peggy Frances helped the customer load the plows and collected the payment for the work. She gave him some fish fresh from the pot after he politely declined the invitation to stay and eat with us.

A nice breeze was stirring, just enough to break the heat. We moved a table into the protective shade of the large red oak. We enjoyed our fish, fried potatoes, fried corn bread and onions while sitting in straight-backed chairs set in a circle. Peggy Frances produced slices of a pound cake and some sliced peaches to top things off.

We talked and laughed as if we didn't have a care in the world. Toby arrived just in time to join us. He was surprised and pleased. He talked about the new house and told me I had to find the time to go see it. I had been planning to do that. The time was near for everyone up and down the valley to take a break and join together for a week of preaching, singing, visiting and eating.

Sukey put plenty of fish in two separate cloth bags and tied their tops together. I draped them across Dutch's back behind the saddle on a piece of clean canvas. I remembered Bobby Jack's story of how Peewee, or "Pete," had been attacked from behind. I wanted my hands free to react to any perceived threat. And, yes, I figured Harland for a back shooter. But why?

It would be dusk by the time I got to the Scroggins barn. I decided to take Rusty and Cajun along. The trip was un-eventful, and all were glad to get the fish. They had already eaten supper, but they discovered a hearty appetite for more. I was tired and sleepy, and it felt good to stretch out on the bed.

The sounds of Rusty and Cajun snarling and barking woke me from a deep sleep. A man's running feet desperately pounded the earth down the road that led to the house. Soon I heard a horse's hooves putting more distance between the culprit and the house. Satisfied that my faithful dogs would keep a sharp lookout, I went back to bed after letting them know that I appreciated them. I slept soundly and awoke feeling well rested.

I remembered Bobby Jack's descriptions of minor defects in the shoes of the horse sold to Harland. That was the horse that carried our intruder back into the valley from the Scroggins place. Upon returning to the house, I looked for boot tracks. I found them underneath a kitchen window. The window had been left partially up, as had several other windows, for the cooler night air to get into the house. What did he have in mind?

The kitchen opened to the north, giving handy access to the barn, and the window was near the back porch. Something shiny glinted underneath the edge of the porch. It was a knife, a skinning knife with a fancy bone handle. It was the kind of knife Harland would choose, although I couldn't imagine him using it to skin an animal. I guessed that Cajun's teeth in his arm had caused him to drop it. .

The knife was not at all necessary to gain entrance, so why did he have it in his hand? There was only one logical conclusion. It was the perfect instrument to cut someone's throat, and it was razor sharp. Except for being sharpened, it showed no evidence of having been used. He must have bought it after he left my home. I believe I would have seen the lump in his clothing if he had carried it on him then, unless he had it in his boot.

A working man never carries a knife in his boot because it is uncomfortable. Moving in shady backstreet dives in a large city might call for different priorities. I had underestimated Harland, and such a mistake can be fatal. He surely intended to kill me. I could reach no other reasonable conclusion. But why?

When I discussed the matter with Brenda Ann, she immediately connected it with Bing. She might be right, and that could be the explanation as to why he had remained in the area. Bing had taken Harland's horse and outfit, but in the dark he probably did not know it was Harland. In his desperation for a horse, he probably didn't care.

I thought of the good time at the impromptu fish fry the previous afternoon, and I wished for that kind of atmosphere to prevail all the time. Living close to the land required daily exertion in order to just survive, but most residents of The Ozarks took the physical demands in stride. They drew pleasure from working so closely with all that God provided in nature.

Pa and Ma had explained to me, and to Betty Jean and Lou Evelyn as well, that there were children of God and children of the devil. "You will always have to deal with the children of the devil," they said. "Don't let them discourage you and take the pleasure of life from you. You need to learn to recognize them. Some of them go to church."

Betty Jean had opened her eyes as to Harland's true nature. That was a really good development. On the other hand, did any of us know his real nature? What was his game? That he was capable of murder, I would not have guessed. When he left, he was angry at Betty Jean. Would he try to harm her? Why was he hanging around?

Like most women in The Ozarks, my sisters knew how to use firearms, but they needed to gain additional skill in their use. Time was marching on, and soon they would be alone at the house unless I moved back home. The thought startled me.

For me to stay at the Scroggins house while I was recovering from my injury was acceptable so long as there were other adults in the house. But as soon as I was well and able, which wasn't far away, it just wouldn't be decent for me to continue to live in the same house with Brenda Ann. I had become accustomed to going and coming, and Dutch probably wouldn't know what to do with himself if he didn't make the daily trip.

So long as Harland and Bing were on the loose, I wouldn't feel right to leave either of the two houses without a man's protection. It was another looming problem that needed a solution. It crossed my mind to go on the hunt for Harland, and for Bing as well if he was still in the area. I made the decision to report Harland's attempted entrance into the Scroggins house to the sheriff so the sheriff could be on the lookout for him.

When I got to my place, Bobby Jack was there. He and Sukey had the same idea. Find Harland. "Pa will let Pete off long enough to find him. We can hogtie him and take him to the sheriff," he said. Bobby Jack was visibly upset and ready to do something.

"Have you made it okay with Peewee to call him 'Pete?'" I asked.

Bobby Jack grinned. "He liked the idea. He said that was what his grandmother called him. He said that being little got him into a lot of fights, and at first he would fight anyone who called him 'Peewee.' But his grandmother told him that most people didn't mean anything bad by it, and that he ought not be so touchy."

The trip to town became unnecessary. The sheriff and a deputy rode up the hill and into the yard within minutes of our conversation. He had with him a picture of Harland. "This is the man who bought that new rifle Bing dropped," he said. "And he came back to buy another one just four days ago. I just got this picture. He's wanted in Springfield for buying and selling stolen goods."

The sheriff paused, obviously waiting for my response. "Sheriff," I said, "that man tried to climb in a window at the Scroggins house last night. My dogs ran him away and he dropped this when they got after him." I walked to Dutch and pulled the skinning knife from the saddle bag.

"Well, how about that?" the sheriff exclaimed as he looked at his deputy. The deputy spoke up.

"I was the one who talked to the mercantile owner over in the next county. This slick-talking cat bought a new saddle, a complete outdoor outfit and some nice clothes. He also bought a big skinning knife and a whet rock to sharpen it. He made the merchant pretty curious as to what he was up to, so he decided he would report it to the sheriff over there. When a deputy showed him a copy of this picture, he recognized him."

"How did you know that he was the one who tried to get into the Scroggins house?" the sheriff asked. "You have been spending the nights there since you messed up your leg, haven't you? Reckon he was trying to kill you for some reason? Maybe he's mixed up with Bing."

"He bought one of the Marlow horses after Bing knocked him off his horse in the middle of the night. Bobby Jack Marlow here, knows the tracks of the horse they sold him. Bing got possession of the rifle we brought you by knocking Harland off his horse. But Harland must have been in a powerful hurry to replace it."

"Harland?" the sheriff responded. "You know his name then. What else do you know about him?"

"I know that he has been a worry to me since last summer when he came here with my sisters. I had bad feelings about him then. But he was sparking Betty Jean and I tried to see him in the best light. He showed up here unexpected last week, and Betty Jean sent him on his way. He left here mad at her and taunting her about a gold wedding band with a big diamond that he had intended to give her."

The womenfolk had gathered on the front porch, and I glanced at Betty Jean. Her face showed a mixture of embarrassment and relief. The sheriff and his deputy looked at one another and began to laugh. After they finished laughing, the deputy explained.

"This cat was pretty talkative when he was buying his outfit, and he wanted the merchant to know that he had plenty of money. He flashed that ring and asked the merchant what he thought of a girl so stupid that she would turn down a ring like that." He looked at the four women on the porch and added. "Whichever one of you it was, I don't think it was stupid. I think you were real smart."

Betty Jean lamented, "No, I was stupid for letting him think I might accept it. I was stupid for not seeing through him at the very first." Peggy Frances put her arms around her and hugged her tightly.

"Won't you men give your saddles a rest and come inside?" I suggested. "Let's put what we know with what you know, and see if we can figure what they are up to.

The deputy obviously liked the suggestion. "The sheriff said that you have some of the coolest and best spring water anywhere in this part of the country. I'm hot and thirsty, and I know the sheriff would like some cool water too." He and the sheriff reined their horses to the hitching rail and dismounted. They loosened their cinch straps.

Lou Evelyn stepped forward. "Will the horses let me lead them to the lot where they can also get some fresh water? They must be thirsty too." Betty Jean walked down the steps to help her sister, and Peggy Frances muttered something about some cake and coffee as she went back into the house.

Peggy Frances had insisted that I work inside. "I don't want to hear a shot and find you lying in a pool of blood," she had told me. "You make an inviting target under that shade tree."

When the sheriff came through the door, the jars of honey and the shipping crates caught his attention. He said, "I can carry a couple of those jars in my saddle bags. I like honey on my biscuits." He was reaching for his wallet as he spoke. The deputy decided that he wanted a couple of jars also.

"I have never seen bee hives like you have. And you have so many of them," said the deputy. "You are a real bee man.

I have heard about your honey production operation. Mr. Scroggins got you started with those new-fangled hives, didn't he?"

"I learned a lot of things from Mr. Scroggins," I answered. "And I really miss him. Yes, he introduced me to the methods used by the Dadant family over in Illinois. This bum leg would have spelled disaster for my honey production operation if it had not been for Brenda Ann Ashley, a great-granddaughter of Mr. and Mrs. Scroggins. I believe she loves working with bees as much as I do."

The sheriff grinned at me with a "Don't try to fool me" look. He grunted, "Couldn't be because she likes the one who owns the hives, now could it?"

Just as I often found words springing out of my mouth without any thought when I talked to or about Brenda Ann, I answered the sheriff without thinking. "Well, Sheriff, I often wonder about that in the middle of the night. She is the kind of person who would help anyone who is down and out like I have been. I can't imagine anything better than for her to see me as more than just someone who needs help."

The sheriff's face assumed a kind and almost fatherly look. "Sometimes a woman is waiting for the right words spoken at the right time in the right way. You might want to rehearse them when you are doing your midnight pondering. A woman likes for a man to speak up."

Peggy Frances was standing behind the sheriff with a pot of coffee in her hand. She looked at me with a half-smile on her face and nodded her head vigorously. Then soundlessly she mouthed, "Dummy!"

The deputy came to my rescue. "When we rode out of town this morning, I certainly didn't expect this kind of treatment," he said. "Coffee and cake in the middle of the morning. That's not usually a part of our day." He directed his remarks at Peggy Frances.

145

The sheriff wanted to find out all about the new house Toby and Peggy Frances were building. He was inquisitive in a friendly and neighborly way about all that was going on with all the families in the community. I realized that there was more in his mind than just casual visiting. For both political and law enforcement purposes, it was his business to stay well informed.

There seemed to be a reluctance on everyone's part to turn to the subject of the meeting. The sheriff was duty-bound to make a sincere effort to apprehend Harland, now that he had received the Wanted poster. Moreover, his first duty was to protect the law-abiding citizens of the county, and I gave him credit for being sincerely committed to the performance of his job. Politically, his more important accomplishment would be the apprehension of Bing.

We all agreed that a search should be mounted for both Bing and Harland. Even if they managed to escape, it denied them a free hand to simply lurk in the shadows and to strike like a copperhead when a person least expected it. I had put my crutch aside and was using a walking stick. The sheriff questioned me as to whether I had recovered enough to assist in a search. "We need some local knowledge of terrain," he said.

"Nobody would be any more help than Pete," Sukey volunteered. "He sees things that nobody else sees. And he will always be the first to hear something moving through the woods." I had noticed an improvement in Sukey's grammar. She was making an effort to speak like Betty Jean and Lou Evelyn.

She paused, and we all waited for her to say more, for it was obvious that she intended to say more. She tried twice to say more as tears welled in her eyes. Finally, gaining control of her emotions, she said "Pete has good reason to catch Bully. Bully has tried to kill him three times."

I was seeing a side of Sukey that I had not seen before. I had become accustomed to her tough, take-it-as-it-comes attitude. Perhaps she and Pete had each experienced so much of the downside of life that she felt special empathy with him. Then again, was there more?

I affirmed what she said about Pete. "I'm thinking that Mr. Marlow will be glad to let him off for a while without docking his pay. He worries about outlaws on his freight runs, and anything he can do to reduce that risk will be to his own benefit."

I looked at Peggy Frances. "What do you think, Peggy Frances?"

"Well, He likes to have him along on his freight runs, for the reasons that Sukey just mentioned," she answered. "But this is a slack season, and he is spacing his runs further apart. There should be time between runs."

"Bing just might leave the country if he knows Pete is actively looking for him," I said. "I believe he is afraid of him. I glanced at his face when he saw Pete waiting for him in the middle of the road. You couldn't find a better picture of stark fear. He couldn't drop his rifle and rein his horse around quickly enough."

"We have the protracted meeting at church coming up three weeks from now," Lou Evelyn said. "It would be nice if people could go and come without worrying about either Bing or Harland. If they are still on the prowl, many people will stay at home with their guns handy."

GOOD VERSUS EVIL

Harland was running scared, scared and unhappy. Since his arrival at the Weber residence, nothing had worked out right. He still couldn't figure what had come over Betty Jean. He had figured her for a simple romantic who he could always manipulate to his liking by dangling some idyllic scenario in front of her. She would believe him, and she would still believe him when he offered excuses for why those wonderful scenarios had not become reality. He could string her along until he was tired of her, and then he would rid himself of her one way or another.

He thought of returning to Springfield. On his own home turf he would feel more confident in dealing with Bing, the man he knew as Johnny Jones. He had all the marks of a dangerous man from his first contact with him, but Harland fancied himself something of a dangerous man himself. He had been called a wizard at quiet knife work by his peers, and he especially liked the fact that quiet knife work didn't draw immediate attention.

When he met Bing at their prearranged meeting place, he found Bing in a vicious mood. When he was foolish enough to point out the fact that Bing was riding his horse, Bing just laughed at him. "So it was you on that horse. I tried to knock your brains out. I'm glad you know how to pick out a good horse. Have you wiped out that Weber kid?"

When Harland told him he had not yet been able to do that, Bing exploded and called him every vile name Harland had ever heard. "I think he's wary of me," Harland protested. "I couldn't talk him into riding anywhere with me."

"If you can't do a simple job, I will just have to start dealing with somebody else," he said. "And I may knock you off just to get you out of the way. You have been shorting me on the price anyway. You are not the only fence around."

Harland had intended to challenge him about the canvas bag he had seen in Rick's possession. He recognized it as the same kind of bag Bing had delivered to him, tied securely in the same kind of way. Considering Bing's threatening attitude, he thought better of it. In fact he was beginning to wonder if he would get away alive anyway. The brute was in a killing mood.

"Look," Bing said, "I'm gonna give you one more chance to get rid of Weber. If you don't deliver, I'm through with you. Now just get your sorry hide out of my sight. I don't want to see you again until you get Weber."

The attack by Rick's dogs shocked Harland to his self-centered core. It was completely unexpected and they meant business. They were not playing with him, and he felt lucky to get away. He had never run so fast and so desperately. He now understood Bing's aversion to taking care of Rick personally.

He wanted and needed to get the next delivery of jewelry in exchange for Rick's demise, but he had begun to wonder if he would actually get the jewels if he succeeded in killing him. At Marlow's place when he bought his horse, he overheard conversation between Marlow and his sons about someone named "Peewee" riding with Rick to the sheriff's office. It seemed that Rick was delivering something very valuable, and they feared that someone might intercept him.

Afraid to show any curiosity, he listened carefully and tried to make sense of what they were saying. Marlow had wanted

Peewee's opinion as to which horse to sell and he was absent. The younger son, who Harland took to be about eleven or twelve years old, seemed to have a good idea of what this "Peewee" thought about all the horses. It surprised Harland that Marlow gave so much weight to the words of a boy.

Harland wondered if somehow "Johnny Jones" had lost possession of the jewels. After all, he had lost his horse somehow, and he made no offer to compensate Harland for taking his horse from him. He seemed to think it was funny, the only time during their meeting that he deviated from his vicious surliness.

He dreaded meeting with the nasty-tempered thief again. Even if he had succeeded in getting Rick, "Jones" might just try to kill him instead of delivering the jewels. And it looked as if he might have lost the jewels. He would not be as easy to kill as the jewel thief might think, but the thief scared him. Maybe he should just go back to Springfield, but when he left, law officers were getting too close for comfort. He really needed this last shipment in order to relocate.

He had intended to take Betty Jean with him. He wanted to separate her from all contact with her family in order to bring her under his complete control. In trying to get everything in order, he had waited a little too long. Somehow Lou Evelyn had gotten to her. He had no doubt that Lou Evelyn was the one who had messed up his plans. She didn't like him.

Knowing what he knew and surmising the rest, he still could not bring himself to leave. Accustomed to success in whatever nefarious plans he sought to carry out, he could not bring himself to accept failure. "Jones" thought he would be easy to knock off, but if he could somehow find him with the jewels, he might knock him off first.

All along he had known that killing Rick would bring a thorough investigation, but if he killed "Jones" and left his body on an Ozark hillside, neither law enforcement officers nor anyone else would likely pursue the matter beyond a perfunctory review of the surface facts. From day to day he just bided his time, hoping for something to break that would enable him to get his hands on some jewelry. He knew from his own surveillance that "Jones" was still in the area, and that must mean that he had something going for him.

In the meanwhile Bing, now using the new moniker, "Johnny Jones" when he rode to get supplies, grew more morose and harsh by the day. He had become a danger to every living creature. A creature of pride like his mother, he had been humiliated almost beyond his ability to bear. He had enough money to go to California and to live for a while, but he wanted to permanently leave the outlaw life. It was hard and he was tired, tired mostly of looking over his shoulder and running scared.

Next to his pride, vengeance motivated Bing. Of course the desire to exact revenge grew out of his pride. If someone did something to hurt his pride, that person had to pay. Nothing had ever hurt his pride like his encounter with the fourteen-year-old Weber kid. After that episode, everything turned sour for him.

The way Weber, at the age of twelve, had immediately singled him out as the one to watch rather than the deputy who was making a move to grab him, had earned Bing's grudging respect. Still, the kid needed to be taught a lesson about pointing a rifle at him. A look at the kid's eyes told him that he would shoot if pushed. The natural way he handled the rifle, like it was an extension of himself, told him that his shot would go true to the intended target.

It would be a small and amusing thing to see the kid cower from his whip, but he didn't cower. He moved forward instead to meet it, snatched it from Bing's grip, and turned the whip on him. For that humiliation, there was only one answer. He had to die.

He waited patiently for the right opportunity. To take him out soon after the encounter would have meant that he, Bing, would become the primary suspect. Even if they didn't have evidence to make it stick, it would bring renewed attention to the humiliation he had suffered. But now he had no patience left. But how? Where? When?

Things had been going so good before the Weber kid fiasco. Mrs. Weber was a most alluring and willing woman. He had plans to get Mr. Robinson out of the picture and to take his place. He had always wanted to be a prominent citizen with power over others. The thought of having people come to him for favors, and to be able to deny them, indulge them or just string them along, fed something deep inside him. He would enjoy having people actually beg him for his good will.

He would be free to insult people, call them names, ridicule them or bestow special favors on them, depending on his mood at the time. He longed for the power to punish those who failed to give him appropriate adulation. Except for that Weber kid, he would now be enjoying that status.

He had always had a way with women, or at least with a certain kind of woman. He had no interest in those who read The Bible and took it seriously. They were a drag, just boring. But now the scar on his face caused the prettiest ones to look elsewhere. When he told them a tale of having gotten the scar in some heroic action, it helped considerably. He would just feel much better when the one responsible for the scar was gone and none of his acquaintances knew the truth.

In order to arrive in California in style, he needed more money. Having learned enough from Yancey to make undetected entries into buildings, he had entered the sheriff's office in search of the jewelry. He found only a list of the contents of the bag signed by a man he remembered, the banker. That put them beyond his reach, and his disappointment was immeasurable. He had already imagined the chagrin of the sheriff when he missed them.

He also entered the Robinson house during daylight hours when the Robinsons and their driver were gone. Knowing the location of Mrs. Robinson's jewelry box, and knowing that she usually kept several impressive pieces of jewelry in it, he hit pay dirt. It was a good haul. Mrs. Robinson immediately suspected Bing, but she had no way of telling anyone of her suspicion without revealing why she suspected him.

Of course, she could easily concoct some farcical reason for suspecting Bing that would leave her innocent and pure. But she had developed the same relationship with their current driver, and Mr. Robinson had become suspicious. He had made no accusation, but he often came home unexpectedly. His demeanor had changed, and she believed that he had hired someone to keep an eye on her, perhaps more than one person.

Bing had not gotten over Mrs. Robinson's contemptuous rejection of him. She led him to believe that he meant more to her than just recreational activity when her husband was away. He had always been the one who callously and casually rejected those who were no longer useful to him. Now that Yancey had dropped him, it somehow brought back the rejection by Mrs. Robinson. He couldn't take out his frustration on them, and he needed an outlet for his pent-up anger produced by their rejection.

He never camped at the same place more than two nights in succession. Yancey had taught him that. Grudgingly, he admitted to himself that he had learned a lot from Yancey. He realized that he had developed reckless and sometimes sloppy habits. Nat, Sukey's man, had often urged the gang to move on when he wanted to spend another two or three nights in the same camp. And they had experienced several close calls because they had not followed Nat's advice.

Somehow Nat had gotten killed, and he gave a lot of thought to making Sukey his own woman. He envied Nat's having such an appealing little woman, and she was an energetic worker. They all enjoyed her good cooking under difficult conditions. Two things gave him pause. First, he didn't know how badly she had been injured when she got shot. Second, and more importantly, he knew she detested him.

He recognized that his pent-up anger and increasing impatience had become a danger to him. He could almost hear

Yancey trying to talk him into a calmer and more thoughtful approach. Most of all, he knew he should put miles behind him and forget all the reasons for his anger. But that prominent scar would go with him, and it would remind him of Weber every time he fingered his beard.

His thought processes seemed to run in circles, and for the first time in his memory he could not make a decision. Consequently, he literally moved in circles from one two-night camp to another. He had every reason to move on to new country far away. Why could he not bring himself to do it? The destination needed to indeed be far away, and that meant that cold weather would be upon him before he arrived.

As each day passed, his horse became more difficult to handle. And in his mind, it was his horse, even though he had knocked the rightful owner out of the saddle in order to take him. In his agitated state, he failed to notice that the poor grazing the horse was getting was not sufficient nourishment. After all, he had bought a sack of oats for him a while back, and he thought that was being especially good to him.

It was more than just the inadequate rations that increasingly bothered the horse. Until Harland bought him he had been well cared for by knowledgeable horsemen, and now he was handled roughly and thoughtlessly. Trained to respond to gentle touches of the reins on his neck, he had to now react to frequent snatches and jerks that made his mouth sore. And he never got the friendly pat combined with a few kind words that he had become accustomed to.

In Bing's mind, the horse was just getting contrary, one more thing to aggravate him. He had not taken the few moments required to check his hooves to make sure all was well. He sometimes made him go long periods of time without water, and expected him to continue the same pace up a slope as on level ground.

The horse's back was getting sore because Bing had let the new saddle blanket get gritty. He never took the time to examine and clean the horse's back. Peewee had done all those things for him, and he was loathe to assume that responsibility now. Most men on the dodge gave careful thought to the condition of their mounts, being keenly aware of their dependence on them. Among the many resentments he held against Mr. Robinson were the times he had been scolded for not giving adequate care to the Robinson horses.

It was time that he make contact with Harland again to jack him up about not doing his job on Weber. He would intimidate him and scare him, but he had lost confidence that he would be able to pull the job off unless he just got lucky. Those cursed dogs. He carefully rode wide of the territory that they covered around the Weber and Scroggins houses, as well as the route between.

Of course, he had no intention of actually compensating Harland for the job. He knew of a couple of places he could conceal a body, and there would be nothing but a skeleton when it was found, if ever. Without a body, the sheriff wouldn't be looking for anyone. And it wasn't as if anyone was likely to connect Harland to him in any way.

With Weber out of the way, he wouldn't worry about Peewee. When he put this part of the country behind him, Peewee couldn't offer up any information that would hurt him. He didn't want to admit to himself that he had a deep fear of Peewee. The little man was super human in many ways. Downright spooky.

As much time as he spent thinking about various aspects of his situation, he gave no thought to an actual systematic search being made for him. He knew that a small posse had gotten on his trail after the attempt to recover the jewelry before it reached the sheriff's office, but he had easily given them the slip.

He gave no thought to the fact that he had eluded them by using methods learned from Peewee. And he gave no thought to the possibility that Peewee might search for and locate his camp. If he had given that possibility any thought, he would have immediately left The Ozarks far behind.

PEOPLE ON THE MOVE

After Sukey suggested that Pete's talents be put to good use to apprehend Bing and Harland, she experienced an emotional upheaval. As a married woman loyal to her husband, Nat, she had never given a thought to any kind of relationship between her and Pete. Even so, a special bond developed between them. The two of them performed all the necessary and mundane tasks required to keep the camp running smoothly. They learned respect for one another in the day-to-day challenges of a sometimes hectic existence.

As she told the sheriff and his deputy of the attempts on Pete's life, she was overcome by emotion. She quietly made a quick and largely unnoticed exit into her bedroom. There she held her head in her hands, and her whole body shook uncontrollably. When she finally regained her self-control, she made a clear and definite decision. She and Pete belonged together. She would act immediately.

Peggy Frances was pouring hot water from the kettle into the dishpan to wash the coffee cups, plates and forks left from the sheriff's visit. Stepping close to her side and looking up at Peggy Frances she spoke in an uncharacteristically husky voice. "I'm going to walk over and see Pete."

Struck by her demeanor and her tone of voice, Peggy Frances showed her concern. "Is something wrong? Are you okay?"

"Everything is alright," she answered, her tone reverting more toward normal. "I just want to talk to him." She didn't tarry for any further exchange of words, but slipped quickly out the door. She left Peggy Frances with a puzzled frown, staring at the door she closed behind her. By the time she finished washing the cups and plates, her woman's intuition told her what was happening.

Sukey found Pete working with the two-year-old gelding recently purchased by Marlow from Clayton Hardeway. When he saw Sukey some distance away, he released the young horse into a stall. When Sukey got within speaking distance, she could see the concern on his face, and she quickly allayed his fears. "Everything's okay," she said. "Nothing's wrong. I just want to talk to you."

She began by commenting on his name. "Peter Cornelius Elliott. That's a good name, a biblical name. And "Pete" is a really good short version. It fits you. I'm glad we made the change."

"I like it too…" He paused instead of speaking her name. "Sukey" is not your real name, is it? Did Nat give you that name?"

Sukey nodded. "My real name is "Miriam," another biblical name. When I was just a girl, I read The Bible quite a lot, and I was proud of that name. I have been reading it quite a bit since I moved in with Toby and Peggy Frances. It's the first time since I married Nat."

"Then that's what I will be calling you," he said. "A name is important. I never did like that other name. It didn't fit you."

Miriam had never been one to play around the edges of a subject, and having made up her mind, she didn't dawdle. Besides, Bobby Jack might show up. She had made up her mind as she walked the mile through the woods that if Bobby Jack was present, she would tell him she had to talk with Pete privately. Bobby Jack had little comprehension of privacy, and he was curious about everything.

Launching very directly into the purpose of her trip, she said, "Pete, you need a woman, and I need a man. Not just anybody. We need one another. We understand one another like no one else can. We have shared some tough times together, and we each learned to put confidence in the other. How do you feel about that?"

Pete was thinking of practical things. Her words were like the music he had learned to love, but better. "You know I sleep in that feed trough," he said. "I have some land, but the house that is on it has a rotted and leaking roof. You know all that. But I know you well enough to know that we will just do what we have to do. We will make it work."

"Shucks, Pete. We have lived for years like varmints in the wild. We know how to survive. And we will do more than survive. We will build us a home and have children. We will put up winter stores like civilized people do, and on those cold winter nights, we will warm ourselves by hot red oak coals in the fireplace."

Pete appeared thoughtful. Miriam continued, "I know this is sudden. What are you thinking, Pete? You are not having second thoughts about it, I hope."

"No, Miriam, but I ain't never had a woman. You are gonna have to help me." Miriam laughed and threw her arms around him. "There's nothing in this world that I would like better than that," she said.

"I was just thinking a few minutes ago about how fast things can change," Pete said. "Just a few weeks ago you and I were living on the dodge with almost no chance for a decent life. Yeah, Miriam, we can do it. I probably couldn't make it with any other woman, and I wouldn't even want to try. Some mules can work together, and some can't. People ain't much different from mules and horses. You and me, we make a pair."

Pete's thoughts were pushing his tongue, and he wasn't ready to quit talking. Miriam remembered Bobby Jack saying that Pete liked to talk when he could ever get started. "I was thinking, Miriam, that for life to have any meaning, a person has to produce something, make something, grow something, build something or help somebody else do it. We lived a life where we stole what someone made or grew. That's just no good, even if you get rich at it."

He continued. "We got caught up in it and didn't give it the thought we should have. But we were the only ones in the gang willing to make something and to take care of what needed care. Now we are free of that, and we need to make the most of it. We can build a home and build a family. We can help build a good community with good neighbors. With God's help, we can do it Miriam."

"I'm ready to tell everybody," Miriam said. "And I will tell them I have left my old life and my old name behind. As soon as we can set things up with the preacher, I will be 'Mrs. Miriam Elliott,' the proud wife of Peter Cornelius Elliott." Pete grinned like he couldn't be more pleased with the dramatic turn in his life.

"That gelding is looking at you like a lost puppy. What do you do to make horses like you so much? Maybe it's the same thing that made me come trotting over here. I'm heading back, and you had better get back to that horse. Come over tonight if you can, and we will sit on the front porch and talk." Without a backward glance she headed for the gate.

At the gate she turned suddenly to see Pete staring after her. "You will probably have the sheriff and a deputy coming to see you, maybe today. Don't get concerned. They want you to help them find Bing and Harland. You be careful."

"That may be them coming across the creek now," Pete answered. "There are two horses." Miriam had not heard the horses. She was reminded again of how he always heard and saw things before anyone else. The thought made her proud.

When she approached the house, Rusty and Cajun met her with wagging tails. Dutch hung his head over the fence and bobbed his head at her. In the calf patch, the new calf ran and played as if he just could not contain his energy. A dove cooed nearby, and a gentle breeze stirred the leaves of the trees. They all served to encourage her optimistic mood. Life was looking better, much better.

By the time she reached the top step, the front door opened. All three of her female house companions were waiting expectantly. Peggy Frances had told Betty Jean and Lou Evelyn where she had gone, and she shared with them her observation that Sukey seemed quite emotional about it.

Miriam stopped as she stepped onto the porch. She paused for effect as they waited. "Just as soon as we can get our ducks in a row, I will become Mrs. Peter Cornelius Elliott." She spoke "Mrs. Cornelius Elliott" as if the words were delicious and invigorating. Her lively eyes and glowing countenance said even more. She was bursting with the good news.

As an afterthought she added, "And 'Sukey' will be a name that I will leave in an unpleasant past. My real name is 'Miriam,' and I was real proud of that name when I was growing up. I will be known as 'Miriam Elliott.' A new name for a new life."

All three rushed to her and hugged her while they gushed forth womanly sounds and platitudes. Rusty and Cajun looked up at them from the yard with puzzled frowns on their canine faces. They were trying to understand what was happening. A red rooster jumped on the lot fence, flapped his wings, stretched his neck and crowed. It was almost as if he did understand.

As Lou Evelyn noticed Dutch's ears pointed toward the south, Cajun and Rusty suddenly bounded in that direction. Hearing their barking, Rick looked up from where he was busy replacing the queen in a hive that suffered from a large drone population. In a better position to see, he called to the dogs, and they quit barking. Unable to leave the hive at that moment, he turned to the women.

"It's the Hardeway girl!" he told them. "She looks to be alone." Betty Jean, Lou Evelyn and Miriam all ran to meet her. Peggy Frances remained watchful at the door. She reached inside with her left hand and rested it on the barrel of the lever action rifle that leaned against the wall. Her eyes searched all the nooks and shadows.

When they reached the girl, she replied to their questions by beginning to cry. "Miss Sukey, I'm sorry," she said between sobs. "I want you and Daddy to get married. I acted real ugly, and now Daddy is so unhappy. He had started to sing and whistle while he worked, and now he's back like he was. I like him when he's happy."

Betty Jean quickly went to Miriam's rescue. "Marrying has to be left between grown folks, Linda Ruth. If your daddy wants a wife, we will find him a wife. You have a real good daddy, and there are good women who would like to marry him. Shucks, I might even be willing to marry him myself."

Linda Ruth was regaining her composure. "But he wanted to marry Miss Sukey. I would like for you to marry him, but he likes Miss Sukey."

She paused to give the matter some thought. "I like Miss Sukey, too, but I was ugly to her." She looked at Miriam. "I'm sorry Miss Sukey. I'm sorry." She looked absolutely pitiful, and Miriam felt torn inside.

"It's okay Linda Ruth. It's okay. Now listen carefully. I love you, and I like your daddy, but I'm promised to another man now." Linda Ruth's lips began to quiver and her eyes to tear up again, but Miriam quickly continued.

"Don't you worry your pretty head even a little bit. Now that your daddy knows that it's okay with you, he will find a good woman. He will find someone to love you and Charlie and make a good home for you. Right now, we have to let your daddy know that you are okay. He must be worried sick about you."

"Daddy and Charlie took the mules and wagon to the back of the place to haul stove wood. I need to get back before they do. I didn't tell him I was coming over here." She hesitated. "I saw a man on a horse, and he scared me. After I crossed the ridge, I looked back and saw him. He was following me. I hid from him."

Miriam's features sharpened. "Can you describe him, Linda Ruth? What did he look like?"

"He is a big man with a dark beard. I got out of his sight by running around the hill, and then I ran down to the creek. I found a place where the bank is washed out and I hid under the overhang. He almost found me. He got real close. He talked real bad. He cussed his horse. If his horse had not been acting up, he might have found me."

"I got a good close-up look at him when I was peeking through some roots," she said. "I could see a bad scar through his beard when the light hit him on the side of his face."

"Why would Bing try to nab a little girl?" Lou Evelyn asked. "You would think he would try to stay out of her sight."

Miriam's eyes flashed with anger. "To use her for bait. That's the way he thinks. That's the way he operates."

"He was mean to his horse," Linda Ruth said. "Daddy says if a man is mean to horses and mules, he will be mean to women and children."

Rick had put the lid back on his hive, and he called to them. "Come on up to the house," he called, "and fill me in on what is going on." He removed his hat and veil, picked up his hive tool and smoker, and limped toward the house on his walking stick.

When Rick gained a full understanding of the situation, he made a decision. First of all, he congratulated Miriam on her pending marriage to Pete, and then he said, "I will ride to tell Clayton that his daughter is safe. All of you hold the fort here. Keep your eyes and ears open and keep Rusty and Cajun close to the house."

Betty Jean handed him a cold biscuit with a thick slice of ham tucked inside, together with his water skin freshly filled with cool spring water. "You will miss the noon meal," she said. "Gotta keep my big brother well nourished. I don't want you to get hungry before you get back."

Rick held Dutch to a steady walk and studied the terrain for likely places for an ambush. Bing might have moved out of the area. Surely he would have surmised that the girl had told her story to adults by this time. But Bing was a puzzle. Why was he hanging around at all? Who could tell what was going through his dark mind?

And Harland. Where was he? And what was he up to? Were the two of them working together? Was anyone else with them? Yes, it was time to roust them out, to bring things to a head and to a conclusion. Sometimes an old wild boar turned mean and dangerous. Men got together, hunted him, and eliminated him.

Dutch stopped, turned his head to the left and cocked both ears in that direction. Rick pulled his rifle from the saddle boot. He and Dutch remained motionless for a half minute, and then Rick heard it. A horse was walking toward them, alternately starting and stopping. It was coming down off the ridge above them. Rick talked in a low tone to Dutch. "Just hold still boy. Keep quiet."

The horse didn't have a rider. When it came into view, Rick could see that although it was a truly fine animal, it was gaunt and suffering from ill care. The horse was having trouble walking without stepping on the reins. He could see the butt of a new-looking Winchester, but with fresh rust on it. Rick needed to make contact with Clayton Hardeway before he panicked over the absence of his daughter. On the other hand, he couldn't leave a wounded man lying on the ground somewhere.

Without leaving the saddle, he tied the reins to a bush and began to backtrack the horse. He cautiously kept watch around him, both front and rear. When he was almost ready to turn back, he looked behind him to see a man untying the horse. Rick recognized Bing Hodges. He was beyond effective rifle range, and Rick watched him mount the horse and ride down the hill toward the creek. He had managed to acquire a new rifle.

To satisfy his curiosity, Rick continued to backtrack the horse. As he suspected, Bing had been thrown from the horse. When a horse is ill-treated, he will sometimes rebel. Somehow Bing had concealed his presence from both Rick and Dutch. Rick had kept his rifle in his right hand ready for action, and that was surely what had kept Bing from taking a pistol shot at him. He would have to remember that Bing was good in the woods.

Clayton Hardeway and his young son, Charlie, had just pulled the wagon alongside the woodpile when Rick arrived. He and Charlie were wondering why Linda Ruth had not met them outside as usual. Seeing Rick on Dutch brought immediate apprehension to Hardeway's face, and Rick spoke quickly to set his mind at ease. "Linda Ruth is fine, and you don't need to scold her. She was just trying to look out for her daddy."

A puzzled expression replaced the apprehension, and Hardeway waited for Rick's explanation while Rick dismounted and gripped his walking stick. "Linda Ruth is at my place. She went over there to apologize to Sukey. Before you get any ideas, Sukey and Peewee are planning to get married, but I left four women who are determined to find you a good wife. Let's get this wood unloaded and those mules unhitched. I'll finish explaining on the front porch."

Charlie started to ask a question, but his father cut him off. "You heard what he said Charlie. We will get the wagon unloaded and the mules in the lot, and then we will talk." He began to toss the wood into a pile on the ground, and Charlie began to stack it.

"Don't worry about stacking it now," Hardeway told him. "Just toss it off the wagon. We will stack it later." With Rick's help, the wagon was soon empty and Clayton jumped into the wagon. He reined the mules under the wagon shed and unhitched them while Rick led Dutch to the hitching rail at the front porch. Clayton soon joined Rick and Charlie on the porch.

"You know, Clayton, women folks, even from the time they are little girls, are sensitive to the moods of those around them. Linda Ruth said that when you began to see Sukey, you began to sing and whistle when you worked, something you had not done since your wife died. When you quit seeing her, you quit singing and whistling and began to act unhappy. She blamed herself and set out to get it straightened out."

"I had no idea," Clayton answered. "I knew she had been especially nice to me lately, cooking me my favorite foods and asking me what she could do for me. I didn't know anything like that was going through her mind. I wouldn't have had her going three miles through those woods for anything in the world. Wild boars and sows with new pigs."

"It was worse than that, Clayton. She had to hide from Bing Hodges. She saw him following her in time to hide under a washed-out creek bank. And I crossed paths with him on the way over here. His horse threw him. He slipped away from me while I backtracked his horse. He's good in the woods. I didn't see him until he was untying his horse, and he was out of rifle range."

"We are going to have to get some men together and find him. We can't put up with him trying to grab our children." Hardeway's face was hard.

"We had a meeting with the sheriff and his chief deputy at my house this morning. He's getting men together to do that. Bing would likely give them the slip except for one thing.

Pete---that's Peewee---Pete can track him down and bring him in. Clayton, that little man doesn't miss a thing that's going on around him. And he's the first to hear or see anything that moves."

"And you say Sukey is going to marry him?"

"Yes, and she doesn't want to be called "Sukey" anymore. That was a name her outlaw husband gave her, and she wants to leave that name in her past. Her name is 'Miriam,' and we are calling her by her real name now."

Clayton looked at his mules rolling in the dust of the lot and it was plain that he was thinking. "Do you think Linda Ruth would be okay with me seeing some other woman?" he asked.

"Her number one concern is that you be happy. She proved that by walking three miles through the woods today, and she intended to walk three miles back." Rick paused and then laughed. Clayton and Charlie looked at him strangely. Charlie was saying nothing at all, but he was hanging on every word.

"I'm laughing because you don't know what kind of a fix you are in, Clayton. I left four women who are determined to find you a good woman. And if I count Linda Ruth, that's five. If you didn't have two children to feed and care for, you could hide in a cave somewhere. But it looks like your bachelor days are about over." Rick listened to a hen singing in the yard while he wondered if he should tell him about another conclusion he had reached. He decided to toss it out for him to consider.

"Unless I miss my guess, Betty Jean would welcome your attention. She was hovering over Linda Ruth like a mother hen, and she told Miriam that she had been jealous of her when you were coming to see her."

Clayton looked startled, and he sat forward in his chair. "I figured she would be going back to Springfield. Do you think she would really be willing to be the wife of an Ozark farmer?

And I know it takes a special woman to take on two growing kids."

"I'm not saying anything more about that Clayton. It's just something for you to think about. You and Charlie had better get a quick bite to eat. You will want to make it back from my place before sundown. Your mules will get a real workout today. With Bing Hodges roaming around and acting crazy, it will be a good idea to bring your guns along. You never know if you will need them."

"I have taught both Linda Ruth and Charlie to shoot," Clayton said. "And to pay attention to what's going on around them. We will be okay. Come on in and eat a bite with us."

The ride back was uneventful. Rick rode well ahead of the wagon because its noise interfered with his ability to hear. When the wagon rattled and clucked into the yard, Linda Ruth ran to meet her Daddy with tears in her eyes. "I'm sorry, Daddy! I just wanted you to be happy. I didn't mean to cause all this trouble."

After Clayton and Charlie assured her that they were not angry with her, she gestured to the four women who were watching from the porch. "They said they are going to find you a wife. Miss Lou Evelyn has a man friend, but Miss Betty Jean said she is still looking."

Clayton looked at Betty Jean with a broad grin on his face. She grinned back. He looked back at Linda Ruth. "Now that sounds interesting, Linda Ruth, plumb interesting. We have had enough excitement for one day, so I'm not going to ask her to marry me today. We had better get you back home."

Rick rode with them almost half of the way and then he waved goodbye as he turned Dutch toward the Scroggins place. He discussed the events of the day with Brenda Ann and found her incredulous that Miriam and Pete could make such a hurried decision to marry. That Clayton could so quickly shift his attention from Miriam to Betty Jean amazed her.

"I'm very happy that Miriam has dropped that nickname for her real one," she said. "I really like 'Miriam.' And that was Pete's idea? There is a lot more to Pete than I ever imagined. More depth. But the way people just up and decide to get married on the spur of the moment here in the hills, is something I can't get my mind around. Can you explain it to me Rick?"

Before Rick had a chance to answer she continued. "For instance, the arrangement with Toby and Peggy Frances was a gift of God to you. And you were the one who suggested it to Toby. Just as soon as they could get to the courthouse and get to the preacher's house, the knot was tied. They are both great people, and I have no doubt they will be loyal and loving for a lifetime, but it's still just astounding." She repeated her question. "Can you explain it Rick?"

Rick's mind was turning. He thought he was gaining some insight into that mysterious reserve Brenda Ann maintained, the thing that kept him from understanding what was in her heart and mind. "Well each case is a little different, Brenda Ann. Toby and Peggy Frances had known one another for most of their lifetimes, and they had each been eyeing the other for quite a while. Other people had noticed it, including her father who wanted to keep her at home for another year or two."

Rick paused, wondering if he should tell her about the desperate early-morning trip Peggy Frances made to his house with a freshly baked cake. He quickly concluded that the purpose of that trip should remain secret forever. "When I suggested to Toby that he go get Peggy Frances and set up housekeeping at my place, I knew it would be like nudging a couple of loose boulders on the edge of a cliff. I knew it was what both of them had wanted for months."

"As to Pete and Miriam, I suspect that if it had been left to Pete, he wouldn't have had the self-confidence to approach Miriam. He has had nothing in his background to suggest to him that a woman might be interested in him in that way.

You have been around Miriam enough to know that she can be sudden and decisive." Brenda Ann was looking at him as if he was imparting knowledge and understanding of a rare sort. Actually, she was thinking that a man just wasn't supposed to have that kind of understanding of human nature.

"You should have been present when Miriam suggested to the sheriff that Peewee, uh Pete, would be the man who could run Bing to ground. She suddenly choked up and went to her room. I could hear her trying to control her sobs. When she came out of the room, she announced that she was going to talk with Pete." Brenda Ann was listening intently, and Rick realized he was enjoying the telling of the story.

"She and Pete had shared the same outlaw camp for more than two years, and from what I can understand, they did all the work around the camp. I really don't believe that Miriam knew that she had those tender feelings for Pete until she told the sheriff that Bing had tried three times to kill him. That's when she choked up. Thinking of the attempts on his life stirred something deep inside her."

"Yes, I can understand how she might act suddenly," Brenda Ann interjected, "but I still have this idea that there should be some meaningful interaction of more than just a practical nature before a man and woman get married." She threw up her hands in a gesture of frustration. "I guess I have read too many stories about princes and princesses."

Rick gave her a mischievous grin. "Well I never read many of those stories, but I seem to recall that some of them got married quite suddenly. A quick marriage and 'They lived happily ever after.' End of story."

Brenda Ann laughed. She was laughing at herself, and Rick laughed with her. The seriousness lifted. The discussion grew lighter. "I suppose life has to be practical," she said. "What makes life worthwhile is doing something worthwhile. I can't begin to tell you how much this summer has meant to me. I have thanked The Lord many times that Gramps taught me enough that I could help you. Now that you have taken the hives over yourself, I'm feeling useless."

She laughed again. "I don't want anything really bad to happen to you, but maybe you could just sprain your ankle so that I could feel needed again."

It was one of those times when the words just spilled out of Rick's mouth without him first giving thought to what he was going to say, or even that he was going to say it at all. His countenance became very serious. A cool breeze had begun to blow out of the valley, relieving the late afternoon heat. A pair of doves swooped down into the yard and began to look for some grain that Brenda often scattered for them. Brenda Ann noticed the change in his countenance, and she waited expectantly.

"I hope this is not too sudden, Brenda Ann. I love you, and I'm *in love* with you. I can't imagine life without you. I want to be a loving husband to you and to make you happy every day of every week. Will you marry me? Will you be my wife?"

A broad grin spread across Brenda Ann's face. "Now *that* is the way you do it Rick. And the answer is 'Yes.' I was beginning to wonder if you had some reservations."

THE CHASE

When word spread through the area that Linda Ruth Hard-eway had been stalked by Bing Hodges and forced to hide from him, the consensus quickly prevailed that immediate action must be taken. The Ozark way of life involved everyone, including women and children, wandering among the hills and streams on a regular basis. It was summertime, and the children swam in cool pools of clear water. The muscadines and pawpaws would soon be ripe, and children would be wandering through the wooded areas to find them.

Residents of the Ozarks from their earliest years were trained and conditioned to deal with the hazards of nature, including panthers, copperhead moccasins, bears and wild boars. They took those dangers in stride as just a part of life. To worry about an evil and half-crazed man who might appear anywhere at any time was another matter. Parents accepted the natural dangers of the Ozarks and trusted their children to cope with them, but this threat was unacceptable and subject to elimination.

It would soon be time for the summer preaching and singing, the time when a visiting preacher would lead daily worship services for a full week. It was a time when families visited with one another and shared meals that had all the nutritional bounty of the Ozarks prepared in every way imaginable.

That special occasion of the year should not be dampened by the fears of aggression by either Bing or Harland.

When the word spread that Harland was also camping alongside springs and streams and that he was wanted in Springfield, almost everyone offered their cooperation to the sheriff in locating and capturing both of them. A network of citizens was organized to assure that any sighting or any other relevant information could be passed along to everyone. Younger children were unhappy at having to stay within sight of an adult, and older children carried a firearm with them when they got out of sight of the house.

Several of the older boys, perhaps braver than they were wise, began to actively search for any sign of the presence of the two villains. Information began to flow back to the sheriff, and they were able to narrow the search. Pete concluded that Harland was attempting to make contact with Bing and that Bing was avoiding that contact. No one understood why Harland didn't just flee the area. In fact, no one understood why either of them didn't just leave.

Actually, neither Bing nor Harland, at this point, posed any serious threat to anyone except to one another. Harland had nursed serious doubts as to whether Bing had any stolen jewelry to pass along to him. He doubted that Bing intended to deliver any such goods to him at Rick's demise, regardless of whether he possessed any jewelry. Having been an accomplished burglar himself, one who was never, so far as he knew, so much as suspected of such activity, he decided to use his skills to burglarize Bing's camp.

He needed everything of value he could acquire in order to leave Missouri behind him. Rather than go west as many fugitives from the law had done, he would go east. He felt more at home in large cities, and he believed he could easily assume a new identity and lose himself in the crowds of a large city. He had discovered that he was wanted by Springfield, Missouri authorities, and it completely surprised and shocked him. The discovery gave urgency to his plans to return to city living.

Like many criminals, Harland had believed that he would be able to ply his trade for a profitable lifetime without ever being caught. Even now, he didn't believe he would be apprehended. On a trip to buy supplies he had begun to enter the store where he had previously purchased what he needed. He imagined that he had developed a special rapport with the storekeeper, and he was grooming him as a source of information. As he reached for the door handle, he saw his picture on a "WANTED" poster.

Finding a place where he could conceal himself and his horse until nightfall, he returned to the store after all the lamps in town had been extinguished. He forced entry at the rear door and quietly gathered enough supplies to last him for a couple of weeks. He knew the burglary would increase the urgency to leave the area. In addition to the storekeeper, all the townspeople would be upset by the burglary. The storekeeper would surely suspect him.

Although the picture on the "WANTED" poster showed him as clean shaven, and he now had a bushy growth of beard, he knew that he was easily recognizable. He played with ideas as to how he could make himself less so. The picture showed him well-groomed and well-dressed with no hat. He would make it a point to wear his hat at all times and to look a bit scruffy. Most importantly, he would show his face only when absolutely necessary.

What worried him most was the necessity to return to Springfield to retrieve the remainder of the jewelry, that which he had not already sold in violation of his agreement with Bing. He also had a stash of cash at a separate location. He congratulated himself for having the foresight to choose locations that could be accessed quickly and easily with minimal observation, although it was not law enforcement officers that he had in mind at the time. He had been thinking of exposure to other criminals.

Harland knew that he would need money on which to live for a lengthy period of time, and he believed that Bing had a substantial sum of money with him. Some quiet knife work would enable him to make a thorough, unhurried search of both his body and his camp. And the chance that there would be a collection of jewelry attracted him so strongly that he simply could not resist making the effort to acquire it.

Having spent years on the dodge, Bing habitually watched his back trail, often circling back to see if anyone had bothered to track him. When Harland picked up Bing's trail, Bing soon picked up on the fact. When Bing made his camp, he anticipated Harland's visit, and he fully expected it to be un- friendly. Although stealthy and quiet in city neighborhoods, Harland had not acquired comparable skills for moving quietly in the woods.

When Bing stretched out on his blankets, he knew Harland was shadowing his camp, and he knew his exact location. He knew that Harland would await his heavy breathing, so he did his best to produce the sounds of a man sound asleep. He had no knowledge of Harland's skills with a knife nor of his propensity to use a knife; but even so, he anticipated a knife attack because he believed Harland would be prudent enough to opt for silence. Gunshots after nightfall attracted attention.

As for Bing, he preferred the risk of attracting unwanted attention to the risks associated with knife play in the dark. He would rely on his Colt 45. He had spread his bedroll in a shallow cave of an otherwise sheer rock wall. The moon was shining from the direction of the only approach and Harland would be silhouetted against the moonlight, while the nook in which he lay was completely shadowed.

When he saw Harland clearly, he could see a knife in his right hand and a pistol in his left. Knowing that Harland could not yet see him in the shadow, he continued his faked audible breathing as he took careful aim. The thought of a bullet ricocheting from the rock walls of the cave made it espe- cially important that Harland not get off a shot. Bing's shot sounded especially loud against those hard walls and Harland crumpled to the ground. The knife and pistol slipped from his grasp.

He held his aim on the still body for a full minute and watched for any signs of life. Venturing closer, he saw that the bullet had entered between the eyes, exactly where he had aimed. He congratulated himself on a perfect shot. Uncharacteristically for him, he resisted the temptation to search the body. He recognized that as it lay, with the two instruments of death inches from his hands, those who found the body would readily see that the killing was an act of self-defense.

Gathering his bedroll, he walked to his horse. He would need to be miles away before anyone investigated the gunshot. In the moments following the gunshot, he heard Harland's horse snort and neigh desperately. Then came the sound of hoof beats as it tore through the woods and up the hill. He would have searched the saddle bags and perhaps taken the horse, but he didn't want a horse that was gun shy.

Pete was awakened by a horse walking up the hill from the direction he had heard a gunshot a couple hours earlier. He rolled out of the feed trough and waited in a shadow just outside of the barn. The saddled horse with no rider walked steadily to the gate and neighed softly. One of the Marlow horses answered.

Pete, while watching and listening with rifle in hand, walked slowly to the gate and opened it. The horse stepped quickly inside. Pete recognized it as the horse sold to Harland. Seeing the remains of a torn bridle with bits and reins missing, he recalled Marlow mentioning that he warned Harland that the horse was terrified of guns. He decided to leave him saddled with the partial bridle in place so that others could see him as he appeared at the gate.

After first loosening the cinch strap, he led the horse to water and he drank thirstily. He put some oat hay, with the grain heads still attached, in a different trough from the one in which he slept. He went back to sleep to the sounds of the

177

horse's teeth grinding the hay. The horse's appearance indicated that he needed the hay. The sheriff and his deputy were to arrive shortly after daybreak to begin a search for Bing and Harland. This would be a good start.

The Marlow house had a long front porch overlooking the valley that separated the Marlow place from the Weber place. At good daybreak, constantly changing clouds of mist hung just above treetop level across the valley. Mrs. Marlow put ham, bacon, scrambled eggs, biscuits, gravy, butter and sorghum syrup on a long table on the porch as the men gathered for breakfast. Claude and Bobby Jack joined the men. A cool breeze stirred, and the morning was very pleasant, even though it would become a hot day.

The sheriff looked across the valley and reminisced. "This takes me back to my growing-up years," he said. "I joined the Union Army when I was seventeen, and I have had little time to just enjoy nature and the beauty of The Ozarks since then. I didn't really appreciate the special appeal of The Ozarks until the war. When we were marching across flatlands and swamps, I began to appreciate what I had left."

After sipping from his coffee cup and munching on a slice of bacon, he continued. "When I got back from the war, I thought about going west, and I also thought about trying to buy a piece of that good farmland I had seen back in Illinois and Indiana. Then the sheriff offered me a job as a deputy, and lawing sort of got into my blood. Things were pretty rough back then, right after the war, and I had the satisfaction of knowing that what I did was very important."

Everyone was inclined to listen, and he enjoyed having a small audience. "Got married after three years when things had gotten settled down a bit. We got us a little house in town close to the courthouse. Our youngest kids are about ready to get out on their own, and I am beginning to feel the long days a little more. Another term or two and I intend to retire to the edge of a valley like this. All the good springs have been taken, but I'm hoping to find one for sale."

The horses were talking to the one that had come back home during the night, and the big mules acquired since its departure were curious. Pete was watching all of them to make sure nothing got out of control. "Now that Weber place," the sheriff continued, "it was one of the first places settled when the land was populated by outlaws and Indians. It was selected for that good spring and the good farmland over the ridge. Plus a good field of fire for defense. Places like that are not available anymore, but I'm asking the Good Lord to help me and the missus find a good place. I'm glad I stayed in The Ozarks, and my wife loves them as much as I do."

The sheriff got serious about putting away his buttered syrup and biscuits, and Pete spoke up. "I'm guessing it was about two hours after I heard that pistol shot that the horse showed up. The sound of the shot was sort of muffled like it might have been in a low spot. We had better ride wary and not get bunched up."

"Do you think you can backtrack that hoss in this dry weather?" the deputy asked.

"It would probably be a waste of time to try," Pete answered. "I believe I can put us pretty near the place the shot was fired, and we can begin to scout around from there."

Bobby Jack said, "We told him that Red Ball was scared of guns. He was so determined to get a horse right then that he didn't care. He's a good horse in every other way. Do you think you can work him out of it Pete?"

"Not likely," Pete answered. "When they develop that fear, it's pretty well permanent. Besides, it's Harland's horse, and he may still be alive. He may be out there somewhere hurt or wounded. Red Ball had to be tethered to something solid, probably a tree, in order for him to tear that bridle apart that way. That means Harland was not in the saddle at the time. We gotta find out what happened to him."

Pete started to say something more, but then he stopped, raised his head a bit, and turned an ear toward the northwest.

179

"Riders coming," he said. No one else heard anything. From long habit he began to look in all directions for any other activity. Presently others heard the trotting horses as well. It was Slingshot, and he was looking for Pete. He did a double take when he saw the sheriff and the deputy.

Slingshot had two good-looking horses following him on lead ropes. "Had a gunfight with Bully a little before daybreak," he said. "He was stubborn. Wouldn't leave until I winged him. He had just roped my best horse when I got out of the house to check on what was disturbing them. I got enough of a look at his horse to know he's in bad condition. Looked half-starved."

"What brought you here, Slingshot?" the sheriff asked. "I didn't know that anybody knew I was here."

"I came to see Peewee. Wanted to warn him. I figure Bully's gonna be stealing a horse somewhere today, and this is the most likely place."

Slingshot looked at Marlow. "I figured to put my horses in with yours and we could all stand watch on 'em. Bully's a crack shot with that rifle, and he put a pair of shots too close for comfort. My shotgun had birdshot in it, and even though I drew blood, I don't figure I did more than make him mad."

Bobby Jack commented on that. "And he will stay mad for a long time. Those birdshot pellets under his skin will worry him when he's awake and when he's asleep. He will be sore in more ways than one."

"Yeah, go ahead and put your hosses in that south lot, Slingshot," Marlow said. "Me and you and the boys will keep an eye on things. Pete's going with the sheriff and the deputy. They have something else to check out."

Slingshot looked puzzled. "Pete?" he questioned.

"That's Peewee," Marlow answered. "That's what we call him now. 'Pete.' Short for his real name, 'Peter.' I sorta doubt Bing will try anything here in broad daylight, but from what you say, he's probably gettin' desperate. A desperate man may do anything."

"Well, we have a job to do, and we had best get on with it," the sheriff said. Mrs. Marlow walked onto the porch to see if anyone needed anything, and the sheriff expressed thanks to her for him and for the deputy. "We didn't expect this," he said, "although people are real good about feeding us when we are riding around the countryside. This was top quality eating, and it gets our day off to a good start."

Pete soon came from the barn with his horse saddled, and he led the three of them down a bridle path that followed the edge of the valley. They carefully maintained no less than forty feet of distance between their mounts. He was the one who spotted the marks left by a running horse coming out of a creek bottom. The trail was not hard to backtrack, and soon they saw the reins and bits hanging from a tree. They tethered their horses to strong hanging limbs and began to scout around on foot, their rifles in their hands.

Pete soon called the officers to see Harland's body. "Looks like Bully set up for him and was waiting for him. Harland would have been silhouetted against the moon, and Bully didn't want to give him a chance to get off a shot."

"How do you know it was Bully?" the deputy asked.

"I saw the tracks of Bully's horse over there." He pointed to the place where Bing had tethered his horse. "And I know how he makes camp," he added.

"Can't charge him for Harland's death," the sheriff said. "It looks like he left the body, gun and knife just as it fell so that we would see how it happened."

"Regardless, it seems like he must be finally leaving the country, judging by the way he was so determined to get one of Slingshot's horses," the deputy opined. "We have evidence to convict him on possession of stolen goods, but that's all we can pin on him now."

Pete turned around to face the deputy, looking him squarely in the face. In a no-nonsense tone he asked, "What about attempted murder? He tried to kill me three times."

"Yeah, that's right," the deputy responded in a voice that betrayed his embarrassment. "I forgot that."

"Well I have not forgotten," Pete spat.

The sheriff broke the awkward silence that followed. Speaking to his deputy he said, "Get your horse. He won't like it, but we will put the body on him after I have searched it."

The sheriff whistled when he unfastened the front of Harland's shirt. "He has a real fat poke," he said. He opened the soft pig leather wallet and grunted. "Small bills, but a passel of them. Big bills attract attention. And it looks like he was greedy enough to try to get more. Greed. Greed has been the ruination of many a man."

A search of his pockets produced a wad of small bills and a wedding band with a large diamond that gave forth glints of blue light as the sheriff examined it. "That must be the one he tried to give the Weber girl," the deputy said.

"Bully wanted anybody who found the body to know that it was self-defense," Pete commented, "so he left the body exactly as it fell. But if he had known that Harland was carrying this kind of booty, he would have taken it. He has misused and used up a good horse, and now that's the big thing on his mind, to get him another horse that he can abuse." There was no quicker way to get on Pete's bad side than to mistreat a horse.

Back at the Marlow residence, Bing was making his try, not knowing that a reception had been prepared for him. He knew that Slingshot had left with his horses, but it did not occur to him that he had gone to the Marlow place. It didn't occur to him that he, Bing, was so predictable. He was just thinking of the most likely place to find a good horse.

He had given no thought as to where Slingshot would take his horses, and on the little used bridle paths that he followed, he had no occasion to see their tracks. Preoccupied with the pain of the shotgun pellets under his skin, he had no taste for a further exchange of gunfire with Slingshot. He would find a horse that he could steal while the owner was not looking.

He had considered that fine looking stallion that the Weber kid rode, but he knew that Weber would never leave his trail if he took that horse. He wanted Weber dead, but he didn't want to tangle with him. He had reached the point that he just wanted to go to some place where no one knew him. And for that he needed a fresh horse.

Not even for a moment did the thought enter his mind that he was already riding a really fine horse, and that except for his ill treatment, the horse would still be taking good care of him. In his warped mind, the horse was used up and he needed a fresh one. As a child, he had heard a man say, "Buy a horse. Kill the horse. Buy another horse." That approach to handling horses made sense to him then, and he simply used horses until he had to get another one. He had the same attitude toward the people who came into his life.

It was Claude who heard the slowly walking horse near the creek. Positioned down the hill from the horse lot, he had aptly selected the most likely place to watch for a horse thief. A strong wind had uprooted a large white oak, but the tree had clung to life with the roots that remained in the ground on the down side. Seated on a boulder, he peered over the huge tree trunk from the shadow of another large tree.

His attention to his surroundings grew ever sharper as he waited for further sounds after the horse quit walking. Then he saw the head of a bearded man appear above the brow of the hill, alternately appearing and disappearing as he moved from tree to tree. His route would take him about twenty-five yards from Claude's position. He was close enough that Claude knew that he should have been hearing his movements, but he did not. He did not know a man could move through a wooded area so quietly, almost as if he were a ghost.

The thought of capturing the scurrilous villain excited him. When Bing was directly in front of him, he drew a bead on his chest and called out to him. "Freeze! Don't move!"

Before the last word was out of his mouth, Bing had his pistol out of the holster. As the barrel pointed in Claude's direction, Claude hurried his shot. Expecting Bing to follow his directions, he was shocked at the speed with which he reacted. Instead of squeezing the trigger as he always did when shooting game, Claude pulled the trigger. His shot went high and to the right.

No sooner had he pulled the trigger than a blow struck him on his right shoulder. His rifle fell from his hand. Two more shots threw bark into his face. His rifle had fallen on the opposite side of the tree trunk, and he realized that he was defenseless. He kept his head down and behind the tree trunk, desperately trying to think of some way to defend himself.

He was relieved when he heard Bing running back down the steep slope, no longer making any effort to be quiet. Blood covered his right arm as he steeled himself against the deep throbbing pain. He heard his father, Bobby Jack and Slingshot moving slowly toward him, forming a skirmish line with thirty to forty yards between them.

The sounds of a running horse came to them from the creek bottom. Claude walked around the upturned roots of the tree on his way to retrieve his rifle. "I let him get away," he lamented. "He winged me, and that knocked the rifle out of my hand." Bobby Jack ran to check his wound. He quickly cut away the bloodied shoulder of his shirt with the sharp blade of his prized pocket knife.

"Gotta get you to the house and get that bleeding stopped," Mr. Marlow said. "You got a nasty wound there. Looks like the bullet bounced off that bone on the top of your shoulder."

"We gotta follow him," Bobby Jack said. "We can't let him get away."

"That's a special kinda job, and it will take a special kinda man to do it," Slingshot said. "He will watch his back-trail and lay for anybody who comes after him. He ain't apt to be took alive."

"Pete could do it, but he's not here. Somebody needs to get on his trail now. He's gotta be stopped." His brother's injury had upset Bobby Jack, and when Bobby Jack was upset, his nature was to take decisive action.

"He will keep," Mr. Marlow told him. "Calm down. We gotta get Claude's shoulder fixed right now. You can help Slingshot keep an eye on the horses. Bing may circle back."

Mrs. Marlow waited anxiously on the porch as her husband and sons came out of the wooded area. Upon seeing Claude's bare bloodied shoulder, her mouth flew open as she sucked in lungs full of air. Her right hand flew to the base of her neck. Then she turned quickly to go back into the house to make preparations to treat his wound.

Slingshot and Bobby Jack assumed positions on opposite sides of the barn. After a couple of minutes, Bobby Jack left his post to climb a nearby tree. It was a tree that he had regularly climbed since he was five years old because he loved the view. The big tall elm gave him a bird's-eye view of the lower lying terrain south and west of the barn. He had used the special perch so often that he built a seat from scrap lumber to make it more comfortable.

Despite the thick foliage of the treetops, there were many places where he could see through to the ground. From a forked limb he had made a cradle for his rifle because he sometimes shot wild hogs from the perch, hogs that tried to steal grain from the domestic animals. He had also killed several deer from his high seat.

He carefully scanned the forest for miles. He knew the places where a bridle path crossed an open spot, and he watched them closely. Judging by the movement of the sun, which steadily changed what he could see among the shadows of the trees, almost an hour had passed since he climbed to his vantage point. Three horses plodded steadily toward the Marlow homestead. As they alternately disappeared and reappeared among the trees, he noticed that one of the horses was being led by a man on foot.

Having quickly concluded that the three were the sheriff, his deputy and Pete, he tried to ascertain why the one rider was walking. After some five minutes, they crossed a sunlit area where he could see clearly. The deputy was walking, and there was a body across his saddle. Then he caught a glimpse of another rider moving to intersect their route.

He watched the progress of all of them as they came closer to the point of intersection. The single rider arrived first and dismounted at a point above the trail. He tethered his horse and moved stealthily on foot down the slope toward the bridle path. The horse side-stepped to an angle that exposed one full side to Bobby Jack's sharp eyes. What he saw brought his head up with a start.

The sun struck the horse at an angle that enabled him to see the animal's wasted condition. Rump bones stood out prominently. The answers to the questions in his mind about the man's movements and intentions became clear. The man was Bing, and he intended to take a horse from the riders he was intercepting. Did he know who he was intercepting? Bobby Jack doubted that he did. If he knew, he would let them pass.

When Bing saw who he was tackling, would he decide not to waylay them? Probably, but he couldn't take the chance. He had to warn Pete and the law officers. By aiming high he could drop two or three rounds into the general vicinity of Bing's location without endangering the others. He could no longer see Bing, and he assumed that he had settled down in his place of ambush.

Working the rifle's lever action, he squeezed off three shots, paused, and then squeezed off three more. Immediately, he called out to Slingshot to explain what he was doing. He had the satisfaction of seeing Bing race to his emaciated horse, and he pushed the poor abused animal to a gallop up a sharp incline. Already attuned to the feelings of animals, Bobby Jack's work with Pete had given him a special feeling for horses.

Bobby Jack had been taught from the time he first began to ride that he should spare his horse on the many upward inclines. Inwardly he felt for the poor horse, and it was reflected in the grimace that pinched his facial features. The all-out gallop up that steep slope would have taxed a horse in good condition, and that horse was clearly starving.

Pete and the law officers knew that the shots were intended as a warning to someone, but beyond that they did not know what to make of them. Perhaps they were a call for help. Bing heard the first bullet cut through the leaves and hit a tree trunk above his head before he heard the shot. Then it was followed by two more that were similarly close. He heard the following three shots as he was running for the horse.

Rick, busy stacking small crates of bottled honey in the wagon for delivery to a neighboring county seat, interpreted the shots as a call for help at the Marlow place. Dutch was already saddled and his rifle was in the saddle boot. Betty Jean, Lou Evelyn and Peggy Frances came to the front porch to listen. They heard nothing more, and they waved to Rick as he headed to the Marlow place.

He used the well-worn bridle path that Peggy Frances and Bobby Jack had used to bring the white-covered three-layer cake that seemed to initiate so much drastic change in their lives. He held Dutch to a walk, avoiding the rocky surfaces on which the ring of the shoes could be heard for long distances. His mind considered the various possibilities as to what he could anticipate at the Marlow place.

The still healing leg kept him from walking more than a short distance, and he didn't want to ride into an ambush. At intervals he spoke a low "whoa" to Dutch, and they just paused to listen and look. Finally, he could hear Bobby Jack's raised voice as he reported to his father and Slingshot from his tree perch. Relaxing a bit, he permitted Dutch to walk a little faster, but he stopped again before crossing the creek. He had detected movement downstream, and Dutch showed special interest in whatever it was.

Not knowing the reason for the shots, Pete, the sheriff and the deputy had formed a wide skirmish line, keeping one another in view. Rick recognized the sheriff, and they exchanged signals with one another, simply pointing toward the Marlow house. Little by little they all four worked their way up the hill to the horse lot, and there Slingshot explained the reason for the shots.

Bobby Jack continued his lookout in the tree.

Startled by the body tied across the deputy's saddle, Rick did not need to be told the identity of the body. The sheriff pulled a new-looking skinning knife from his saddle bags. "Looks just like the knife you found beneath the window," the sheriff said. "I believe we have solved three murders for the Springfield police, people whose throats were cut by a burglar as they slept in their beds. They were all older people of means who were living alone."

"He was a city guy out of his element," Pete said. "Bully was a light sleeper who studied his back-trail and all his surroundings before he bedded down for the night. He knew Harland was out there."

"What do you think we should do now?" the sheriff asked Pete. "You have a very personal interest in seeing that Bully---Bing--- is caught. But I don't want to see anybody killed while doing it."

Rick took personal satisfaction in seeing the sheriff ask Pete's advice. The little man who everyone had discounted as mentally challenged just needed an opportunity to demonstrate his strengths and abilities. Bobby Jack had been the first to realize that there was much more to Pete than anyone imagined. Perhaps Miriam knew, but like Pete, her personal development had also been stifled.

"Well, he needs to be caught in order to keep him from killing innocent people," Pete answered. "Can't blame him for killing Harland, but Bully will carry a grudge for years, and his answer is to kill whoever he hates. Sooner or later he will probably circle back to take out me and Rick."

The sheriff could see that Pete was thinking, and he waited for Pete to suggest a way to apprehend the fugitive. "He's on a horse that is spent. I just hope he don't kill him. He don't know how to take care of a horse, and he don't want to know. When Bobby Jack dropped that hot lead around him, he took out like a coyote my grandmother threw scalding hot water on. He was about to grab a setting hen under the kitchen steps. Bully slipped and fell twice as he scrambled up the incline to his horse, and then he made the poor horse run all-out up a steep slope."

Pete looked up to see Bobby Jack climbing down from the tree, and then he continued. "My thinking is this: We need to keep him from getting another horse. Get the word out to keep people out of the woods and off the roads. He will shoot a man off his horse if that's what it takes. Everybody needs to get their horses in the lot and set a watch on them, especially after nightfall. Bobby Jack can give us an idea of where he is now, and we can begin to haze him and keep him from resting."

"That will be dangerous," said the sheriff. "I want everybody to stay out of gun range and then pull off at dusk. If we lose him during the night, we will pick him up somewhere tomorrow."

"He likes to move at night," Pete said. "And for a big man, he can move real quiet. He's not going to bed down for the night. He will try to get a horse somewhere."

Bobby Jack joined the circle and added some information. "He got up on that little bald over in the southwest, and he got a good look at the three of you. He probably knows who you are and what he's dealing with. The last I could see of him, he was headed toward the Bledsoe place."

"That Bledsoe stallion is one of the best horses around these parts," Marlow said. "Bledsoe gets a nice-sized stud fee for his services, and people are willing to pay it. That's the only horse Bledsoe has, and I sorta doubt anybody but Bledsoe could ride him. Or even get a saddle on him as far as that's concerned. But he needs to be warned."

"Marlow, if you will transport this body to town, I will see to it that the county pays you for it. It won't be a lot, but it's better than nothing. I think the three of us will wait for Bing at Bledsoe's place. We will scatter out and watch the different approaches." The sheriff turned to Rick. "Would you like to come along, Rick?"

"I think I will spread the word to the other homes in the area, Sheriff," Rick replied. "He was headed for the Bledsoe place when Bobby Jack last saw him, but he may change direction. He has roamed these parts for years, and he knows the lay of the land. If he wants to get out of the country as soon as possible, the Bledsoe place is a loop out of the way."

Pete indicated his agreement with Rick. He looked at the sheriff. "You and the deputy will be enough to set up at Bledsoe's place. I'm going to see if I can pick up Bully's trail and worry him a little."

In the meanwhile, Bing had in fact made a ninety degree turn to the right from his course toward the Bledsoe place. Not out of any feeling for his horse, he had begun to walk the horse and even to dismount on the steeper slopes.

After the sprint from Bobby Jack's bullets, that had come altogether too close, the horse had begun to tremble. And he still had occasional times when his skin twitched uncontrollably. Bing feared being left afoot if he did not carefully manage the small reserve of strength left in the horse. The thought of getting another horse burned on his brain, and he could think of little else.

His changed course took him by a spring at which he had often watered and camped. He gave his horse a rest and an opportunity to graze on a long abandoned meadow that had bushes gradually crowding out the grass. While he watched and listened, he scraped the mold off a piece of ham and ate. Then he washed a handful of yellow corn meal down his throat.

He sat on the ground, leaned back against a tree and considered his situation. He was leaving this part of the country and this uncomfortable outdoor life. All he needed was a fresh horse, and as for any unfortunate fools who got in his way… Well, it was just their tough luck. He would get a fresh horse, and he knew ways to shake off pursuers. Although he didn't have the money he had aimed for, he had a decent grubstake, and he knew how to get more.

Less than an hour after he left the spring, Pete stood on the same ground examining the signs. He saw the scrapings of the mold from the ham, and he saw a bit of spilled corn meal. He took satisfaction in knowing that the horse had gotten a short rest and a few bites to eat. The grass was lush and green, and the water was good.

After a heavy rain, this valley flowed with rushing water. Otherwise some settler would have claimed the spring to make his home. The fact that Bully had actually dismounted on the steep slopes told him that the horse was near collapse. That was the only thing that would have prompted Bully to spare the horse.

Two miles away Bing was checking out a filly in a small meadow when he saw a saddled horse tethered to a tree limb in the front yard of the house. When he worked his way closer, he recognized the horse. It was the Weber boy's stallion. He recklessly formed a plan of action. If the girl was riding the stallion, he would take her with him for a short distance. If Weber was riding the horse, he would kill him.

With that horse, he would put all pursuit well behind him. Remembering Nat's words of caution, he would not keep the horse but sell him for a nice price. By the time the horse became known, he would be long gone. When he recognized Rick's voice inside, he felt a surge of disappointment. He had hoped it would be the girl. Then the malice he felt for Rick surged past the disappointment, and he approached the front steps with his pistol in his hand.

Dutch became suspicious. Becoming disturbed by the stealthy movements of this strange man, he snorted. Bing cursed under his breath and waited for Rick to come to the door. Rick was in the one bedroom of the house talking to the disabled owner, who lay on the bed with a freshly broken leg. His face was etched in pain. A newborn baby slept contentedly in a neatly constructed cradle by his side. His young wife had ridden to town for the doctor.

Rick's pistol was in his hand without his even realizing that he had reached for it. A soft summer breeze blew through the one front window that opened on the porch. The wood shutters had been tied back. Rick stepped slowly to where he could see Dutch through that window and by seeing where the stallion focused his attention, he knew where Bing was. And he felt sure it was Bing. Anyone else would have announced his presence.

He knew that Bing waited for him to appear in the doorway. He would just wait him out. Dutch would let him know if he moved. Cursing under his breath again, Bing backed away from the porch toward Dutch. His pistol remained trained on the open door. Rick watched him with keen interest when he saw Bing's left hand pull the slip knot and release the reins from the hanging limb. He believed that he knew what would happen next.

Unwilling to holster his pistol, Bing's efforts to get the reins on opposite sides of Dutch's neck were awkward and clumsy. Suddenly Dutch snorted and reared up, his forefeet striking out at the strange would-be rider. His left hoof struck the left side of Bing's face and opened a gash down his left jaw to match the scar on the other jaw.

The blow knocked him onto his back, his legs rising into the air above him. He clung to his pistol and his grip on it caused him to inadvertently fire it. A pair of startled hens squawked and went flying through the air. A small limb fell from the tree above. Dutch backed away several body lengths, the reins trailing.

Bing leaped to his feet and fired a shot through the open door as he ran. The bullet cut a hole in the top of a heavy stave of the wooden water bucket setting on a shelf that was mounted on the back wall of the front room. The misshapen slug dented the stave on the opposite side of the bucket and dropped into the water. Forgetting his weak leg, Rick sprang onto the porch ready to get off a shot at the fleeing Bing, but he was putting the smokehouse between him and any pursuer. Then he was gone into a wooded area.

Holding his pistol ready to fire, Rick held his position while listening to the young father trying to quiet the awakened baby. Then he heard the steps of a horse walking away. It just wasn't in Bing's nature to flee so slowly and deliberately. His horse must, indeed, be in a very weak condition. Going back inside, he assured the young father that he would stay with him until his wife returned. Otherwise, Bing might return to get the pretty young filly in the small pasture behind the house.

Pete heard the two shots, and he wondered if Bing had succeeded in getting a new mount. Following Bing's trail, he was aiming directly toward the location of the pistol shots. From his time with the outlaw gang, he knew that Bing was following a route that was familiar to both of them. He stepped up his pace a bit and considered the points at which Bing would likely check his back-trail.

The two pistol shots may have had nothing to do with Bing, and in that case Bing would probably be farther ahead. He would be far enough away that he would not be disturbed by the shots. Pete would soon know. He dismounted and led his horse up a steep grade to a point at which he could see up to two miles ahead. Barely able to see the farm from which the shots had come, all looked peaceful. Then about a half mile from the house he saw movement among the trees.

Intermittently watching for further movement while searching the terrain in all directions, he patiently waited for a clear view of whatever was moving away from him at almost a mile distance. Finally at an open space among the trees, he saw a man leading a horse. He felt sure that it was Bing, still stuck with his weakened and starving horse. He mounted his horse and worked his way at an angle back to the bridle path.

Knowing that Bing had no place for another couple of miles to see him from a distance, he stepped up his pace, closing the gap between them. He wanted to make contact with him before sunset. Plenty of time remained. He remembered that about five miles ahead, there was another likely place to steal a horse, and he was sure that Bing remembered.

He also recalled that a cliff rose vertically over a hundred feet above the valley on the back side of that farm, extending for almost a half mile. The usual route the gang traveled followed a dim bridle path along the top of the cliff. They always paused there to study their back-trail as well as what was happening all about the countryside. About halfway along the cliff, they had to ride away from the cliff to go around a cut that angled down from the cliff to the valley floor below.

Pete anticipated that Bing would repeat that same routine and then ride down the cut to steal a horse from the farm. He wanted to arrive in time to prevent that theft. He would find a place within rifle range where he would be able to see Bing as he conducted his surveillance of the valley. It was no part of Pete's makeup as a man to shoot anyone --- even a man who had tried to kill him --- from ambush. Nevertheless, he would disturb him enough to cause him to ride on.

It was not a part of Bing's makeup as a man to accept responsibility for his own failures, and at this moment, he was cursing his bad luck. His jaw hurt, and blood still trickled down his neck as sweat hindered the natural clotting process. Again, it was that cursed Weber kid and his horse. He would have another bad scar on his face. Sooner or later he would kill that kid. It would probably be later because he had to get established somewhere far away.

He might hire someone to take care of the job. That would be the best way. One thing was for sure; he would not forget. If he had to wear those scars for the rest of his life, then that Weber kid had to die. That would make it a lot easier to live with the scars.

It was not a part of Bing's thinking to weigh the risks of failure. He would get a horse; he would succeed in getting out of The Ozarks; and he would find a way to become wealthy. He would buy whatever he wanted, including women, and he would run roughshod over anyone who got in his way. If necessary, he would kill anyone who threatened the success of his ambitions. He did not think of them as "ambitions." They were definite "plans."

The bridle path that he was following forked, the dimmer fork leading up a gradual slope to the top of the cliff. As he directed his starving horse up the slope, he noticed that the horse occasionally trembled. Not wanting the horse to collapse before he got another one, he dismounted and led the gelding up the slope. By the time he reached the top, his own legs were feeling weak, and he was breathing deeply.

Pete arrived at his vantage point just in time to see Bing reach his position. It was the same that the gang had used several times. It was barely in effective rifle range, especially having to deal with a hundred-plus feet of additional elevation.

Pete tethered his horse out of view behind a grove of young sassafras trees. On the right side of the grove, he found a shadowed place where he could use a large sapling for a rest for his rifle.

Bing stood alongside the bowed head of his horse looking across the valley. The scene appeared innocent, even idyllic, but Pete knew the malicious nature of the man who stood there. And he knew exactly what he intended to do. Few people could afford to lose a good horse, and regret ate at Pete daily for the role he had played in stealing horses.

The gang members, except for Bing, had bragged on him for his skill in getting horses to willingly come with him. Even though he knew it was wrong, he had a feeling of camaraderie and belonging that had been sorely missing in his life. He enjoyed accepting and discharging responsibility, and the other gang members were only too willing to let him assume the responsibility.

All of them except Miriam. Miriam carried her share of the load and more. Recognizing the load she carried, he helped her in every way he could. That he was now going to marry Miriam still seemed unreal, almost too good to be true. They understood one another as no one else could. That she had sought him out with the suggestion that they marry, did wonders for his morale. He truly had something to live for, a good life for the two of them together.

Taking aim at an imaginary target about two feet in front of Bing, and allowing for the increased elevation, he squeezed the trigger of his rifle. Quickly levering another round into the barrel, he sent another one well in front of him for good measure. Bing didn't wait for the second shot. Wheeling quickly, he sprang into the saddle. At that moment he made a fatal mistake, but in his mind he just had another stroke of bad luck.

The horse had become conditioned to rapid getaways, with him furnishing the horsepower to make it rapid. In his equine brain he recalled the strain and stress of those getaways. When he felt the pain in his mouth as he was roughly plow-reined to the right simultaneously with the sharp kicks in his flanks, everything in him rebelled this time. He had tried to cooperate with this rough and inconsiderate master, giving him all he had to give. But no more.

He would not expend his waning strength in another galloping run. Instead, he put all his remaining strength into getting the abusive rider off his back. The harsh pull of the reins had turned his head down and to the right. The starving horse's body continued the twisting turn as his rump and heels flew upward. The increased weight that was thrust onto his forelegs caused the left foreleg to collapse, and Bing's big body hurtled forward and down by the horse's falling neck.

He desperately grabbed at a straggly cedar bush growing on the edge of the cliff as his feet and legs dropped over the edge. His weight was too much for the bush and it broke, barely slowing the motion of his falling and rolling body. As his body fell into the open space and began the sickening descent to the rocks below, Pete heard an agonizing yell. He could understand a few words mixed into the blood-curdling scream. Bing was cursing his luck.

As he fell, his body twisting and turning, Pete could see Bing shaking his fist as he continued to curse. At about two thirds of the distance to the ground, the body struck a protrusion of rock from the cliff, and it bounced outward away from the rock wall. The yelling and arm activity ceased.

As Pete watched the seemingly slow descent of the body, his attention never left the horse. It had almost followed Bing over the precipice, but it struggled to its feet. It swayed in its tracks and then began to amble away from the cliff while occasionally stepping on its reins. Knowing that Bing would be not only dead, but also mutilated on the rocks, he mounted his horse and circled back to begin the ascent to the top of the cliff.

As it ever was with Pete and horses, the horse knew he had found a friend. He kept nuzzling Pete as Pete checked his condition. Knowing the tough time the horse had experienced, he did not discourage him. Harland had bought a very good horse, and it showed even through his emaciated frame. Pete looked forward to nursing it back to good health.

Rick had heard the two shots fired by Pete, and he knew he needed to investigate. Although there could be myriad reasons for the shots, in his gut he believed Pete had caught up with Bing. Remembering how Pete had placed special emphasis on Bing's habit of watching his back-trail, he worried that Bing may have fired the shots at Pete. Looking through the front window, Rick saw a young woman with a rifle move quickly from one tree to another. She waited there while studying the house.

Speaking to the injured man he said, "I believe your wife is back, and she probably heard the shots. Now she sees a strange horse in the yard and she is behind a tree with a rifle in her hands. Does that sound like your wife?"

"Yes it does," he answered. "Is she close enough to hear me if I call out to her?'

"I believe so," Rick said, "although I hate for you to disturb the baby again."

"It can't be helped. I can get her settled down again." He patted the baby on the shoulder and tried to reassure her before he yelled. "Come on in May Ellen! It's okay! That horse is Dutch, Rick Weber's stallion."

Pete and Rick were each glad to see that the other was safe. Rick agreed to stand watch over the gory remains until Pete could contact the sheriff at the Bledsoe place. Although the sheriff and his deputy were both experienced and competent law enforcement officers, they stood with their mouths gaping wide in astonishment when Pete led the bony horse into the Bledsoe yard and told them Bing was dead.

Pete made it alright to leave the gelding at the Bledsoe farm for a couple days before requiring him to make the trip to the

Marlow place. He looked as if he didn't have another mile in him on this day. The men lamented over how a really fine horse had suffered such ill treatment. All agreed the horse should now belong to Pete, and that he was the right man to help the animal recover from the abuse. It became obvious that a bond had already developed between the two of them.

CHANGED LIVES

Brenda Ann and I still talk about that spring and summer, the spring and summer of ninety-one. So many things happened so quickly, things which drastically altered our lives and the lives of several people close to us. We were all young and trying to get started in life. Of course the crucial decision at that time of life is the choice of a mate, the one to become that special lifetime partner.

There comes a time in early adulthood when the mating instinct takes control of young men and women. For some it comes sooner than for others, and it is more, much more, than simple physical attraction. Oh, I know that there are exceptions, especially for brutish and selfish people. And even Jesus the Christ said that some people are not meant to be married. But for the overwhelming majority of decent people, there comes a time to mate, a time to find that one lifetime partner of the opposite sex.

When Peggy Frances walked a mile along a bridle path carrying a three-layer cake covered with white icing, that mating urge was pushing her really strong. Toby was like a blue-hot piece of metal out of the forge he worked, ready to be struck and shaped by the skilled stroke of the smithy's hammer. When from my bed of pain and disability I suggested to him at a midnight hour that he claim Peggy Frances as his bride, he didn't dawdle. At daybreak he was knocking on the door of the Marlow residence.

I desperately needed someone to care for the homestead Ma and Pa had left to my two sisters and me. Toby and Peggy Frances needed a house in which to begin their life together. I couldn't have made a better deal with better people. When Miriam showed up under dubious circumstances, they showed their depth of character by taking her in and nursing her through the wound-healing process. And also through hurts that cannot be seen with the naked eye.

They found themselves with a full house when Betty Jean and Lou Evelyn arrived. Four women in the same kitchen is a prescription for trouble, but if they ever had any serious disagreements, I never knew about it. Even so, the obvious eagerness of Peggy Frances to move into her own new home told me that she and Toby needed some privacy. How many marriages have started under conditions similar to theirs?

The doctor cautioned me against carrying more than twenty-five pounds for several more weeks. He said I could probably count on a lifetime with a crooked lower leg if I failed to follow his instructions. A crooked leg would likely produce a knee problem in later years. When Toby was loading and moving his blacksmithing equipment to his new home, I felt almost useless. Almost everything associated with a blacksmithing operation is heavy.

We had developed the habits of caution during the previous months of lurking danger, and those habits would stay with us for a lifetime. Even though we knew of no threats after the deaths of Harland and Bing, we continued to pause in our work to look and listen. We changed positions so as to know what was happening in every direction. Our eyes examined shadows and watched for furtive movements.

The four women, all strong and able, willingly pitched in to help. Among other heavy objects, they lifted a large cast iron wash pot into the wagon. A new cooking pot already hung in the newly constructed fireplace. Toby and Peggy Frances had accumulated various household furnishings over the months since their hastily arranged marriage, some of which were at the new house and others in my barn.

The Marlows gave a Jersey milk cow to the couple, as did Toby's parents. Bobby Jack promised to give them a puppy from his bulldog. Cajun had just fathered the puppies and now came the three and one-half month wait for their birth and weaning. As soon as the chicken house was finished, laying hens would be moved. It had to be made secure from foxes, owls and other night-time predators.

Toby and Peggy Frances promised a pig roast when cool weather arrived for all who would come. Clayton Hardeway had begun to play a mean fiddle after he began to court Betty Jean. After the death of his wife, he had put it on a shelf and let it gather dust. When Betty Jean saw it and asked about it, he tuned it, tightened the bow, applied the resin and delighted them all, especially Linda Ruth, with beautiful music. He agreed to furnish music for the gathering, and I would join him with my harmonica. If Pete could find a ukulele for Miriam, she would join in. Even though the roast was still weeks away, we all talked about it with keen anticipation.

Betty Jean had taken to the Hardeway kids, and they showed pure excitement over her. Linda Ruth began to ask her father questions that showed her impatience with the courting process. She was ready for Betty Jean to move in. When Clayton told her that adults needed time to talk through some things and reach agreements on certain matters, she volunteered her services in that connection. She believed that she could get everything settled in a single afternoon.

Aunt Carrie and her two daughters inquired about the prolonged stay of Betty Jean and Lou Evelyn, and they experienced mixed emotions when they learned that budding romances explained the delay. The deaths of Harland and Bing made big news in Springfield, and our kinfolks were curious to learn more details of all that had been going on with their Weber kin.

We had barely gotten Toby and Peggy Frances settled into their new home when the annual August meeting began at the church. It seemed that everyone, young and old, loved to sing, and we enjoyed energy-filled harmony with words that told of a promised land for all who would follow Jesus. The church had just acquired new shape-note books containing some new songs to learn.

The women prepared an abundance of good food, each woman apparently trying to out-do the others in preparing delicious dishes. The preachers made long and earnest pleas for everyone to look beyond this life, and to get ready to make that unavoidable transition at the end of this life's way.

There was time to talk. Most Ozarkers were isolated on their individual homesteads day after day. When the opportunity came to visit with their neighbors, they took full advantage of it, and they simply sat and talked for hours. The growing boys spent long afternoons in cool pools of water at the creek. Muscadines were ripe, and the boys competed with raccoons and opossums for them. After eating all they wanted at the vine-covered trees, they brought sacks of muscadines to their mothers so they could make muscadine jam.

Near the end of the revival services, we had two surprise visitors who tingled our ears, touched our hearts, and set tongues aflutter. Our guest preacher had learned that Miss Carson had been our spinster schoolmarm for several years. She had taught me for two years. The preacher gave her and the man with her ample time to give their personal testimonies. First, Miss Carson announced that she would not be coming back for the upcoming school term. It was a decision that she had made only a week before.

Her announcement saddened us because we had all learned to love her, and during school term, she was very much a part of our community. She went back to the home of her parents in Springfield between terms. It was the reason that she gave which started tongues wagging. We had all assumed that she was committed to a spinster life, but she was getting married.

Miss Carson was a very attractive woman and several local men had tried to win her favor. When not one of them met with even the slightest success, people assumed that she was simply not interested in men. Her testimony and that of her male companion gave a complete explanation for her long-standing dedication to the spinster status, and for her reasons for changing.

The daughter of a locksmith, she had fallen in love with an apt and considerate young man who came to work for her father as an apprentice. Her heart was broken and she lost confidence in men when he was arrested for a string of burglaries. She visited him in jail, at which time he apologized to her and told her to forget him. He freely admitted his guilt and offered no excuses for his criminal conduct.

She could not forget him, and she could not generate any interest in any other man. She resigned herself to life as an unmarried woman. Since she loved children, but would not have any, she decided to become a schoolmarm where she could work with them and help them grow up.

Several weeks before she had chanced to meet her old heart-throb on the street. Even though he was older and had disguised himself, she knew him instantly. They both stopped and stood transfixed as they looked at one another. Yancey --- that was his name --- began to sob uncontrollably. She insisted that he go with her to her parents' home, where he repeatedly apologized to them all.

He told them of how he had returned to his old ways as soon as he was released from prison, that he even had some loot stowed away at that very moment. Something --- he didn't know what --- had caused him to become deeply sorry for all the wrong he had done. He had decided to turn in his loot and to return to jail. Seeing Judy Nell Carson on the street made him realize how much he had lost because of his wrongdoing.

What bothered him most was not the price he would have to pay for his wrongs. It was the hurt he had caused others for which no recompense could be made. Miss Carson's father advised him not to be hasty, but to permit him to talk with an attorney about the best way to handle the situation.

"I understand that you want to come clean, Yancey," he said, "and that's what we all want, but you still have some negotiating power where the consequences are concerned. I don't want to see you spend the rest of your life behind bars when you have repented of your sins."

As Yancey talked of how he had returned to safe-cracking, he mentioned the name of the fence they used. Miss Carson told of how she looked at her father, and he at her, with knowing looks. Harland was one of their clients, and they had suspected that he was into shady activities. She told of how he had paid a nice sum of money for two padlocks that would be especially difficult to pick or to break.

He was a talkative sort, and he gave out information that he really didn't intend to divulge. He didn't give people credit for being able to connect bits and pieces of information he provided at different times. Miss Carson and her father put their heads together and decided they could probably determine the locations of the two locks. The next day they found them.

They went with Yancey to the office of a lawyer whose services Miss Carson and her father had used in times past. "Let me talk with the prosecutors in each county," he said. "It will take a few days. Their major concern will be recovering as much of the valuables as they can. Before I talk with them, let's contact the local prosecutor and law enforcement officers. We will get the judge to issue an order to break those locks and see what is behind them."

Being a schoolmarm, Miss Carson knew how to tell a story full of details. She held the congregation spellbound. She told of their suspicions being confirmed by discovering most of the loot at one location and a sizable amount of cash at the other. The cash had been divided into two packets, one of small bills and the other of large bills. Law enforcement officials seemed especially happy at the discovery.

The prosecutor remembered Yancey from the time he was apprehended before his prison term. He remembered his humble acceptance of his arrest and his full cooperation with law enforcement officials. He also remembered the good words spoken for him by Mr. Carson before sentence was imposed by the judge. He told Yancey's attorney that he would recommend to the prosecutors in the other counties that no charges be filed against Yancey.

The lawyer put his other business on hold and took two fast horses on a quick circuit ride of the different counties, meeting with the sheriff and the prosecutor in each county. By alternating between the two horses, he made the circuit very quickly. Miss Carson gladly paid his fee from her savings. As a conservative spinster, she had spent very little of her earnings from teaching school.

Knowing that under the circumstances Yancey would not ask her to marry him, she told him: "We are going to take up where we left off when you messed up. It's past! It's done! We have survived, and we are back together. We are still young enough to make a life together. We are going to get on with it," She sounded every bit like the schoolmarm who had taught me and some other unruly boys for two years.

When Yancey stood before the congregation, he would not permit Miss Carson to sit down. He wanted her to stand beside him. His words were few and direct. "I didn't know what made me suddenly hate everything I had become and decide to turn myself in to the law. I didn't want the stuff I had stolen, and I wanted to get it back to the people I had stolen it from, as much of it as I had left."

He paused, struggling to control his voice. "I didn't know what made me feel that way then, but I do now. God can get hold of a man and change him. I never read The Bible. Jesus was just a man religious people liked to talk about. Judy Nell and I have been reading The Bible a long time every day, and

what I have learned about Him has made a completely different man of me. He died for me, and I want to live for Him."

Turning to Miss Carson, the tall slender former thief looked
long at her. Then he turned to face the congregation again.
"I had no thought at all of meeting Judy Nell on the street
that day. If I had seen her in time, I would have avoided her.
I would have dodged her some kind of way. When I realized
who she was, I was paralyzed. I couldn't move, and I couldn't
say anything. When she spoke my name, I began to cry like
a baby. I don't remember ever crying before, even as a small
child."

"It was like I was full of something that had to come out," he
continued. "I couldn't stop bawling. She took me by the arm
and led me to her home like a lost sheep. God put her on
that street for me. It couldn't be any other way."

The congregation sat so quietly that not even one of the small
children made a sound. He looked again at Miss Carson, and
as if speaking to her and wanting her approval, he concluded,
"I guess that's all I've got to say."

Knowing the power of the testimony the congregation had
heard, and seeing their reaction to it, the visiting preacher
preached the shortest sermon I have ever heard. When the
invitation was given, five rowdy teenage boys stumbled awk-
wardly down the aisle with tears streaming down their cheeks.
Everyone felt that the boys had come to church only to see
the girls and to create some kind of disturbance. Others, male
and female, old and young, followed. People in the community still talk about the revival of ninety-one.

I got a great deal of personal satisfaction at seeing almost all
of the jewelry returned to the rightful owners. My integrity
had been questioned by two couples whose safes were opened
on the last foray by Yancey and Bing. Having recovered half
of the loot when Bing killed his horse from heat exhaustion,
they voiced suspicions that I had withheld the rest of the
jewelry.

When Yancey delivered the other half to the Springfield authorities, together with information as to where it was stolen, my good name had been cleared. The local sheriff shamed the couples for their accusations and suggested rather sternly that they should each match the reward given by the couple who had accepted my account of what had happened. Having been firmly taught by Brenda Ann the difference between being independent and being bull-headed, I gratefully accepted the rewards. They would mean a lot to us.

I had deliberately accumulated too many hives in one location for several reasons, one of which was to maintain the ability to protect them from bears and human marauders. With the additional funds, I could get Toby to build iron cages for some of the hives, and I would reach agreements with homeowners to put other hives close enough to their dwellings that they could keep an eye on them for me. I would begin construction of a honey house for the processing and bottling of the honey. The thought of a well-equipped workspace made me feel good.

Shortly after Bing's death, Pete received a special visit from the sheriff and his deputy. A sizable reward had been posted for Bing's apprehension, and Mr. Robinson was one of the key persons in getting the reward money together from victims. On the premises of the Robinson house, Bing had retied a seldom-used gate in a peculiar way that Robinson recognized as Bing's doing.

Pete and Miriam had made arrangements to purchase an old Conestoga wagon and to have Toby repair it for them. The wagon had not been used for many years, but it had been sheltered from the weather during that time. The owner was willing to let them pay for it over a two-year period, but now they would have the money to immediately pay for it and buy a good a team of big mules to pull it.

The wagon would be used as their living quarters, quarters that could be moved between the Marlow place and Pete's inherited property as work requirements demanded. Having lived on the move with nothing more than minimal camping equipment, they were excited to acquire the wagon. Miriam joked about sleeping in the horse trough, if necessary. Toby was giving top priority to the repair work on the wagon. They ordered a custom-made canvas cover from one of the old-time outfitters in St. Louis.

With all the talk about so many people getting married at once, excitement began to build throughout the community, especially among the women. Even though Miss Carson and Yancey planned to make their home in Springfield, they had decided to marry in our community church building. Former pupils who had moved from the community vowed to come back for the marriage ceremony.

During her tenure as our schoolmarm, Miss Carson had hired local carpenters to build for her a picturesque little cabin near the creek above a stretch of rapids. She loved to watch the water rushing over the rocks and to go to sleep by the sound of it. She and Yancey would spend time there when Yancey could get away from his locksmith work with her father.

After the singing, preaching, eating, visiting and all-around excitement of the summer church meeting, everyone turned to the serious business of gathering crops and making all the due preparations for winter. Winters in the Ozarks could be mild or they could be long and harsh. Sometimes we were snowed-in and icebound for lengthy periods. In particular, it could be hard on livestock.

Preparation was the key to surviving a winter without undue hardship. Stores of food for both people and animals, together with ample stocks of firewood, made for enjoyable times even through the harshest winters. It was a time to visit with one another at the fireside while shaping wooden handles, working with leather, sharpening cutting tools, and mending clothing. A neighbor might drop by to visit at any time, knowing that he was more than welcome to enjoy a meal with the family.

Fall days were almost always quite pleasant outside, and that is where most people were found during daylight hours, hard at work. There had been just enough rain at just the right time to make a bumper corn crop in ninety-one, and the corn cribs filled up quickly. My leg had healed enough to permit me to gather my corn alone, except for occasional help from Lou Evelyn. Betty Jean helped Clayton with fall harvest.

Accustomed to working alone, I gained real satisfaction in harnessing the mules and working them to the wagon. I no longer was dependent on others for the basic things I had always just taken for granted. And I realized now, owing in no small part to Brenda Ann's coaching, that a person can be too independent-minded. The inescapable truth is that we are all dependent on one another.

In the Apostle Paul's letter to the Galatians, sixth chapter and second verse, he said "Bear ye one another's burdens." Then in the fifth verse he said, "For every man shall bear his own burden." I had puzzled over those two verses, unable to resolve the apparent contradiction. After suffering through my disability, forced to depend upon others, I now understood what Paul was telling the Galatians. There will always come a time when one must call upon someone else for help, but in the meanwhile a person should provide for himself while looking for an opportunity to help someone else.

Brenda Ann spent most of her time in and around the Scroggins house, and I joined her when I could. She and her cousins had been quite industrious through the summer months, and there were dry beans, pumpkins, sorghum and corn to be gathered. We would live in the Scroggins house after our marriage until we could build us a place of our own.

Discussions were ongoing among the relatives about selling to Brenda Ann and me all the Scroggins land except a small tract where the house stood. Being near, we could protect and care for the house during the weeks and months when none of the Scroggins descendants were present. We were to have all the time we needed to build the home of our dreams. I could not be marrying into a better family.

Betty Jean and I reached an agreement with Barney and Lou Evelyn to sell to them our interests in our inherited property. They would pay us over a period of three years, to be extended to five years in the event of bad crop years. Barney and Lou Evelyn bubbled with excitement. Having been so closely attached to my parents' home, one of the best farms in the county, I felt a certain sadness. But it was washed away by a flood of gladness, gladness for them and for myself.

I don't know who had the idea. The entire church was abuzz over five couples getting married at almost the same time. The idea may have originated with the pastor. It would save time for him to unite all five couples in a joint ceremony. The idea circulated through the community before we who were getting married knew of it.

Toby found me sawing firewood with my one-man saw. Although I was not to lift any of the heavy blocks, I could saw them and split them. Some of the blocks could be split with an axe, but many of them required a wedge and eight-pound sledge hammer. After my forced inactivity, this was just the kind of work I needed to get back in decent physical condition. After all, I wanted to be in good physical condition when I got married.

"Alright," said Toby with a grin. "It's your time. You pushed me into tying the knot, and now I am pushing you. You have been just too all-fired independent all these years. It's time you had to answer to a woman. What's the holdup?"

I was caught unprepared, and in spite of the smile, I knew he was only half joking. "I had a feeling you would get back at me sooner or later," I answered. "Is that why you looked me up out here in the woods?" Cajun and Rusty came running to greet Toby, interrupting our verbal exchange for a few moments.

When he looked back at me after rough-housing with the dogs briefly, his face was serious. "It seems that a self-appointed committee of women at the church has made some plans for you and the other four couples who are getting hitched up. They want to make one big event of all five marriages. They want you to all marry at one time, and we will have dinner on the grounds after the joint ceremony."

"And you got appointed as messenger boy? Do I have any choice if I expect to live in peace with my neighbors for the next fifty years?"

"You were always good at sizing up a situation pretty quickly," he dead-panned. "No, you don't have a choice. Peggy Frances is talking with Brenda Ann now. You are just as good as hog-tied already."

I looked at Toby seriously. "One thing I'm going to insist upon. I'm going to choose my best man. And that man is Toby Barrett."

He extended his right hand to me. "You got it, man." My right hand gripped his, and what that grip conveyed could not be expressed in words.

I knew that the only thing I needed to do about the wedding was to show up with my hair trimmed and combed, and wearing what I was told to wear. It was not a time to dwell on the merits of independence. Since Ma and Pa had left for that better land, I had always decided where and when I was going and when I would get back. Those days were gone, and I just couldn't seem to generate any regret about that loss of freedom.

After Toby straddled his horse and rode away, I sat on a stump and rested my game leg. My thoughts retraced the hectic developments of the past months. I realized that except for my broken leg, I would surely have let Brenda Ann go back to Springfield, and we would have shared only fleeting greetings when she came to vacation in our rocky hills.

She had maintained a certain reserve that kept me from pursuing her affections more aggressively. When I spoke about that to her, she said that I was so much a son of the hills and streams that she did not know if I would be happy with a girl from the city. She also wanted to know that I truly loved her, that my feelings were more than just the fascination that God gave a young man for a young woman.

Then she turned the tables and told me that she knew that I had not been ready to commit. "Growing up alone as you have," she said, "you also maintain a reserve that I believe will always be a part of you. You finally let me break through, and I like that trait in you now."

I remember how she paused and looked at me seriously, but with a half-smile. "But if you ever shut me out again, I am going to be all over you like a stream of upset bees from a hive you have accidentally kicked."

If Mr. Scroggins had not taught her to work with bees, where would she be now? If I had not been ambushed and came back in the dark of night with a busted leg, where would she be? If Peggy Frances had not come that very morning with the three-layer cake… If, if, if…I thought of the verse in the eighth chapter of Romans that says, "And we know that all things work together for good to them that love God, to them who are the called according to his purpose."

Wagons, surreys and horses came from all directions on the big day. We ran out of space to put the food on the tables. Some men pulled the frames off four wagons and rolled them around to serve as extra tables. Many of the townsfolk were there, including the sheriff and his deputy. Some of them had never seen Pete clean and well-dressed, and I overheard expressions of disbelief. Pete had become a local hero.

One of the proudest and happiest persons attending was Bobby Jack. Pete tagged him to be his best man, and Bobby Jack loved the role he had been chosen to play. Mr. Marlow, a natural supervisor, made sure everything came together as it should. He chided Peggy Frances. "I would have done something like this for you if you had not run off." She smiled and kissed him on the cheek.

Insofar as I could tell, no one held it against Pete, Miriam and Yancey that they had been outlaws. They had sincerely turned from their errant ways, and that was what counted. From personal acquaintance, they knew that Pete and Miriam were new and different people, and they took Miss Carson's word where Yancey was concerned. Miss Carson's word carried a lot of weight with everyone in the community. And they now had an explanation as to why such a lovely and personable woman had chosen not to marry.

Marriage was serious business to the preacher. He reminded everyone in attendance of its crucial importance to society as a whole, but especially to the children born in each marriage. He urged everyone to enjoy the occasion, but to remember the seriousness of it. He reminded each of us who were making the big step into married bliss that it would not all be bliss.

We were warned that there would be challenging and possibly bitterly trying days ahead. "When those days come, you must stand together. You are each a pair joined together, not by me, but by God. You must stand as one with and in God. No problem, no challenge is too big for God." The grip of Brenda Ann's hand in mine tightened as the preacher spoke those words. Although we had not then been joined in marriage, we had already faced some stiff challenges together. I had often expressed my thanks to God and to her.

We rode back to the Scroggins house in the rear seat of the Ashley surrey. Two really beautiful bay Morgan horses pulled it handily across the streams and over the ridges. Mr. Ashley joked that he would now permit us to share the same bedroom. Mrs. Ashley seriously promised not to be a meddling mother-in-law. I thanked Mr. Ashley again for setting the broken bone of my wounded leg. Without his knowledge of such injuries gained in the horror of war, I might now be using a peg leg.

When I began to help take the harnesses from the sweating horses, Mr. Ashley would not permit it. "You take care of my daughter. I will take care of these horses," he said very firmly. "This is your day and hers. Don't worry. I will give you plenty of opportunities to help in months and years to come."

Putting my arm around Brenda Ann's shoulder, I pointed and told her, "Let's walk out there." We walked the one hundred yards from the barn to the headstone that marked the interment of the bodies of Mr. and Mrs. Scroggins. I was well aware that they were not there, that they were very much alive in that wonderful land of promise. But I remembered Brenda Ann speaking to me there after the casket of Mr. Scroggins had been covered with dirt and then with flowers.

I remembered her voice that afternoon from behind me and to my right. "Do you feel alone Rick?" It was almost as if she could see my heart and read my mind. I was no longer alone. In addition to all the other things Mr. and Mrs. Scroggins had given me, they had given me this ever-amazing descendant, this remarkable woman, to be my partner in life. My loneliness had been concluded in the most satisfying way imaginable. It's good not to be too independent.